THE
COMPLEX
LAW

Book Two of THE COMPLEX TRILOGY

HEATHER HAYES

First soft back edition October 2018

Published by AH Digital FX Studios, INC 10/19/2018
AH Digital FX Studios, INC
10551 E. Ririe Hwy.
Idaho Falls, ID 83401
www.ahfx.net

ISBN: 978-1-945597-07-7

Library of Congress Control Number: 2018912585

Cover by Adam Hayes
Book Layout & Design by Adam Hayes

Paperback printed in United States of America

For Connor and Haley
Thanks for giving so much of your time to
help this trilogy become a reality.

Chapter 1

BAM. BAM. "ELIRA, HURRY UP so we can go to
bed," my best friend, Avra, calls through the bathroom door.
Okay, okay. Which of these bottles of soap should I use? I can't
stand here undecided in the shower all night long, so I choose
the green bottle with exotic looking fruit on it. Ooh, it smells
heavenly.

I've never been in such an exquisite shower before. Fancy
gray and white tiles surround me in a beautiful pattern. A
cascade of warm water falls on my head from I'm not sure
where in the ceiling. A sigh escapes my lips as the dirt and blood

my body has collected tonight melts off and disappears down the drain.

My broken toes sting more and more as I stand there enjoying the smell of exotic fruit. I need to get off my feet. When I turn the intricately carved handle in the shower, the water stops raining on my head. I make sure to wipe down the beautiful walls as I leave. I don't want to leave any of my grime behind.

This stunning bathroom is connected to an equally stunning bedroom that Avra and I will be sharing. I can't believe this magnificence is just for our personal use. I think of the two large, sterile bathrooms in the glass dorm, and the sixty girls who share them, unaware of what they're missing. I thought the glass dorm bathrooms were beautiful the first time I saw them. I sigh at how narrow my perception of the world was a few short months ago. I wiggle into the pink thing I find on the bathroom counter. It feels so smooth and silky. My fingers fidget with the edge of the silky... nightgown, as Florence Hamble, my—mother called it. I still can't believe the lovely woman who owns this house gave birth to me. Whew, at least I'm clean now. I won't leave a trail of blood on her beautiful carpets.

"What's taking you so long, Elira?" Avra, calls out.

"Coming," I say through a mouthful of toothpaste. After I spit and leave the bathroom, I hobble into the bedroom and collapse on the softest bed that I have ever laid upon. It is like sleeping on a bed made of fluffy clouds. Avra plops down on the other end. My outstretched hand tries to find her, but she's too far away to reach. This bed is that big.

"How do I smell, Avra?"

Sniff, sniff. "Fruity and amazing." I have to agree; my skin is soft and radiant. I don't know what all the soaps and scrubby things in the shower are, but wow, they worked magic on me after a jaunt into a dirty laundry bin and a garbage truck.

Avra sighs as she sinks into our cloud-like bed. "Elira, your parents are rich."

The fine furnishings in our new bedroom seem to nod in agreement. "I know. I can't believe it. I always thought they had given up everything to get me a spot at the complex. I assumed they were either living in poverty or dead."

Avra takes a bottle of sweet smelling lotion from the bedside table and rubs some of it into her dry hands. "So, are you mad that the government took you away from all of this and stuck you in the complex?" Her slippery hands gesture to the lavish furnishings around us.

I trace my fingers over the elaborately-carved, glossy headboard above our heads. "Hmm." These things are nice. "Avra, all of this stuff is here now, but it could be gone tomorrow. I'm mostly upset that I lost so many years loving and being loved by my mother. I have no memories of her, except for today."

Avra nods. "She is beautiful. I thought a princess was

3

welcoming us to her castle when we walked in the back door tonight."

I smile as I remember my first impression of my mother, Florence Elira Hamble. "You know, Avra, I bet I would be completely different if I had spent my days sleeping on clouds and eating grapes off silver trays." I point at the tray on my bedside table that has actual grapes on it.

Avra plucks a big, purple grape off the bunch and pops it in her mouth. "I'd be mad about losing all of this if I were you." She scoots across the enormous bed to squeeze my hand. I'm glad she still has energy to talk to me after all we've been through in the last few hours; maybe the adrenaline hasn't worn off. Avra was amazing tonight. She lays back on a stack of fluffy pillows and takes in our surroundings. "I love the way your mom decorated this room. It's like she knew you'd come back, and she wanted you to know how much you were missed." There is a note of longing in her voice.

My parents could have easily moved on, but there are pictures of baby and toddler Elira with her raccoon eye, all over this room. My view from this bed is of my name in purple painted decoratively on the wall and pictures of little me surrounding it. The picture of my mom hugging toddler me cheek-to-cheek is particularly poignant. "I can't believe she didn't forget about me after 14 years."

Avra gives me a serious look. "You two have so much to catch up on. You could go out there and start right now."

I cover my yawn and shake my head. "No. My mother is right. I need sleep before we catch up; plus, I feel—nervous around her."

"She's a stranger to you right now, but she won't be for long." Avra stands up and walks to a picture on the wall of baby Elira being hugged by a man with a similar face shape and coloring as me. He doesn't look ashamed or repulsed by my purple raccoon eye. "Your dad looks nice."

I get off my fluffy bed and limp to join her by the picture. "Yeah." My eyes are drawn to the father I haven't met. "He's a doctor." He is away at a conference tonight, whatever that is, but he'll be back tomorrow. "I can't wait to meet him."

Avra is getting tired; I can see it in her eyes. I also sense a touch of jealousy radiating from her as she asks, "Do you think both of my parents are still alive?"

I realize that our conversations tonight have been all about me, yet my sweet friend has lost just as much as I have the last 14 years. "Yeah. Well—I hope so. I will help you find them, Avra."

My friend frowns at me. "They didn't join your mom and Ernestine in the plan to get us back. What if they were happy to get rid of me?"

I can't imagine such a thing. "They weren't happy to get rid of you. I know it. Mentor Maxine told me that only cruel parents are happy to have their children taken away. We'll find them, and I'm sure they'll welcome you home with open arms too." Avra looks like she has doubts. "Hey, even if they don't want you back, we are a family. We will figure out this new world together."

"Who's we?"

"Oh, you know, the first complex escapees in 40 years."

Avra smiles. "Ha, ha! We did do that tonight, didn't we?" She surprises me with a hug. "Thanks, Elira." Her bottom lip trembles. "I'm sorry I didn't believe what the complex actually is at first. You really did save my life today."

She pulls back from me and I blush at the magnitude of her compliment. "What are friends for?" My broken toes are throbbing and Avra is trembling, so I lead her to sit on the end of the bed with me. "I am *your* crazy person after all." Ow, my body. Maybe I should have accepted the pain pills my mother offered me.

She smiles and sighs. "Do you think the boys are doing okay in their rooms?"

I think of the amazement the boys had on their faces when they saw where they will be staying. "I'm sure Ernestine is enjoying every minute with Rocky." Her son was surprised that she wanted to share her room with him. Her dedication to get him back saved us tonight. "Rocky and Ernestine will probably stay up all night talking. They have years to catch up on."

Avra finds a big knot in her wet hair, so she slides off the bed, picks a silver brush off the vanity and starts brushing her hair again. "Yeah. Ernestine is a dedicated mother. We would've been goners without her van." She sets the silver brush down and looks at herself in the mirror, tilting her head to the side. "How do you think the other boys are doing?"

"You mean Scott?"

She smiles and nods. "Yeah."

I imagine the boys looking at all of the fine furnishings of this gigantic house the same way we have. "Our boys are probably thrilled to share a room with only two others instead of 15. Honestly, I'm glad Scott is in there with the twins. I'm afraid those two might be at each other's throats right now."

Avra stifles a laugh. "Yeah, they are fighting over you like I told you they would."

My heart thuds harder than usual in my chest. "I know. What should I do?"

She raises her eyebrows at me. "You should choose between them, so they can start acting like brothers again instead of rivals."

"You make it sound so easy."

She smiles as she sits on the bed again. "You're making it harder than it has to be."

I scowl at my best friend. "How many hearts have you broken lately?"

Avra thinks about that for a second, then cringes in sympathy. "Are you leaning toward one of them over the other yet?"

I think about the last week and nod. "Jefrey has done

nothing but get on my nerves since we planned this escape. I understand his fear, but I need him to be stronger than his fears. Garth—waited for me in the garbage truck and carried me when my foot couldn't run."

"Do you love him?"

"I—I didn't even say who I'm leaning towards yet."

Avra leans back and giggles. "You didn't have to say it. I can tell."

My eyebrows scrunch together in frustration. "I don't know if we really understand what love is. We've read about it in a few books, but the complex was a loveless place. How can we know if we get it right?"

Avra rubs her cold feet then climbs under the covers. "Remember the book *Cinderella*? I see Mentor Roberta as my evil step-mother, Julie and Mara as my evil step-sisters, and Scott as my handsome prince! The way he makes me feel has to be love!"

I can't help but laugh. "So, it's as easy as that, huh?"

"Yep. If you could hold Garth's hand right now, would you?"

I look down at my empty hands. "Yes," I say sheepishly.

"I knew it. It's thrilling, isn't it? No wonder the complex keeps the boys and girls separated by glass. Poor Shasta and Tessa will never know what it's like." Yeah. I realize now how unfair things are for them. Avra gives me a hard nudge. "Make sure you hold Garth's hand tomorrow."

I imagine all of us sitting on the comfortable sofas and chairs in the big room out there. Jefrey might throw something if he sees me take Garth's hand. "I—I will hold his hand while my dad, the doctor, fixes us up tomorrow." *Yawn.* "I hope his ear will be okay; there was so much blood running down his neck..." I unconsciously grab the neck of my nightgown as I remember Garth's blood running down his neck and soaking into my jumpsuit as I laid my head on his shoulder.

Avra pulls my hand off my nightgown. "Garth won't feel a thing if you're holding his hand." A secret delight creeps into her eyes. "Your dad is a doctor. You never liked doctors in the complex. How funny."

I smile at the irony. "I know. Make sure he knows what medicine you usually take and have him listen to your heart. I didn't risk my life to get you out just to have you die out here."

My friend shrugs. "Okay, not a problem. I'm not afraid of doctors." *Yawn.*

Sigh. I have parents. Two of them. I had no idea just yesterday. My hand wanders to the raised purple birthmark around my eye. My fingers follow the shape of it. "Avra, my mother—she is so beautiful. Do you think she's ashamed of the way I look?"

Avra yawns and looks at the digital clock on the bedside table. It says 3:45 am. "Obviously not, Elira. She wouldn't have spent 14 years paying Ernestine to get you out and made this safehouse for you if she was ashamed of you."

Avra has a point. Relief washes over me. "Okay, you're probably right."

"My mother on the other hand... We know nothing about her."

I nod. "We have a lot of parents to look up." I join her under the covers. "I say we start with yours."

"Thank you."

My eyelids are getting heavy. "No problem. I just wish, *yawn*, I could disguise myself better."

"Your mom said we are going to get new haircuts and disguises tomorrow."

My eyes won't open anymore. "Good, I'm glad someone is on top of things. *Yawn*. Will you turn off the light? I need to sleep."

"Sure. Good night, Elira."

"Good night, Avra."

Chapter 2

SNIFF. SNIFF. MY NOSE WAKES ME UP the next morning. Bacon, eggs, and something sweet overpowers my senses and makes my fancy, cloud-like bed suddenly less appealing to my sore body. The clock on the bedside table says 11:10 am. I guess there isn't much morning left. I hope they didn't throw away my victuals. I slip out of bed and stretch. Ow, ow, ow! My toes and my back hurt. Well, to be completely honest with myself, everything hurts. The only thing that doesn't hurt is my head. I have been so stressed out lately. It's wonderful to have the mental strain over with. I can let

Ernestine and my mother take over the decision making for a while. We're all out, Rocky and I have found our mothers, and we are in a nice house with, from the smell of it, delicious food to eat. I think of the five apples that Garth had stuffed in his jumpsuit and the broken-down shack I thought we'd be staying in, and feel grateful.

The full-length mirror on the back of the door draws my eyes to it. Ugh. I've definitely looked better. My eyes are puffy and my swollen toes are the same purple color as the unique birthmark around my left eye. This nightgown is rather... sheer. I'm amazed at how much of my body is revealed through it. I can't let the boys see me in this. Just the thought makes me shiver.

"Elira, look in here. How will we ever choose what to wear?" Avra giggles as she leaves the closet with something yellow and heads to the bathroom to try it on.

The closet in my room is so big; I walk inside of it like it is its own room. The sheer number of colorful clothes hanging in here is overwhelming. I have never worn anything but jumpsuits. My hand shakes a little as I pull each hanger out and look at the beautiful clothes hanging from them. There are tops with separate bottoms, flowing long tube things, like the one my mother wore last night, and attractive leg-hugging things. I'm used to solid colors, but these clothes have many colors and designs. My eye is drawn to a white top thing with blue flowers on it. When I pull it down to examine it, I'm afraid it will be too small for me. Oh well, I'll just choose one of these other hundreds of things... There is a wall in the closet just for shoes, socks and underwear. To think, I was planning on wearing the same three jumpsuits for the rest of my life. What should I wear? I don't know if I should match a top with a bottom, or if I should make them completely different... I will need my mom to help me figure this out later. I take one of the long tube things off a hanger and slip it over my head. It is a breathtaking deep purple color and flows around my legs, bouncing in a fun way. I cringe as I pull on some shoes that match the purple color and try not to tip over. "Ow!" My broken toes don't appreciate being shoved into shoes with heels. "Ah! Ow." These are almost the shortest heels in here, but they are much taller than I'm used to and the pain in my toes is too much to bear. I kick them off and wobble out of the closet to get Avra's opinion.

"Wow! You look so pretty, Elira!"

I pull some of the tube's fabric away from my leg. "Thank you. Do you think these things are for every day, or just special occasions?"

"Who knows? I want to wear one too!"

I see a handwritten note stuck to the closet door. "My mother says that the clothes in the closet are all for us. We can pick whatever we want. I think I'm going to look for shoes with flat heels and open toes. Ow!"

Avra picks out a pretty pink tube outfit. The pink against her brown skin is stunning. We brush our hair in front of the mirror in our extravagant bathroom. I look at the little doodads in one of the drawers; I'm sure we are supposed to put them in our hair somehow. I pick up a pink one and bend it, pop! It opens up like a mouth. I let the little mouth bite into Avra's hair and bend it back the way it was. Ha! It's staying! Avra makes a purple one bite into my hair. Well, this is as fancy as I know how to make us. I'll need my mother's help with these hair things too.

We walk out of our bedroom into the common room. All of the boys are sitting at the table on the left end of the big room. They look, different. The new clothes they're wearing make them look—handsome! The boys' mouths drop open when they see us. I feel heat bursting from my cheeks. I like the attention but feel like they should stop staring now, too. We walk to the table and sit down in the two empty chairs left for us. I sit between Garth and my mother. My mother wraps her arms around me and squeezes me like her life depends on it. She doesn't let go until I squeeze her back. That was—nice. As I straighten myself in my chair, my knee bumps into Garth. I turn red and feel sweat start to form on my forehead. I've never eaten victuals next to a boy before. The proximity is unsettling.

Garth can't keep his eyes off me. "Good morning, Elira. You look beautiful." How did I live 16 years of my life without hearing a voice as appealing as his?

"Yes, you do," Jefrey says across the table with a much louder tone.

My mother looks at Garth and me curiously and clears her throat. "Yes, Elira. You look like a Hamble now that you're out of that horrible jumpsuit." She looks down at the portion of my leg that is showing and jumps back. "I—I will teach you girls what socks, tights, and nylons to wear with your dresses. And, I'll acquaint you with the razors in your bathroom."

My stomach drops. I knew it, she is ashamed of me. I look at her apologetically. "This is a dress? I'm sorry I didn't know I needed something else to wear with it. I've never worn one before, but I love it. Thank you, Mother."

My mother nods and asks to be excused as she rushes out of the room crying.

I look at Ernestine questioningly and ask, "Did I do something wrong?"

Ernestine swallows and shakes her head without looking at me. "No, child. She can't imagine the way you have been brought up. She's sad that you don't know what a dress is and such. Don't worry about it. It will take time to learn each other's language, if you know what I mean. Get yourself a waffle and some bacon and eggs."

"I—Okay." My mouth waters as I take in all the food on the table. "I'm so glad I didn't miss the morning victuals. They smell amazing."

Garth smiles at me and loads up my plate. I am relieved that his ear is covered up with a bandage; I don't want to relive it getting shot last night.

I am mesmerized by the plentiful golden-brown syrup that is puddling around my waffle. I've never had so much delicious sweetness before. It brings a memory from the complex to mind. "I made a waffle once. It didn't look near as tasty as this one does though." I take a bite of the beautiful golden circle covered in little square pits. "Mmm, this waffle and the syrup are delicious."

Ernestine smiles a crooked-teethed smile at me. "They really are; your mother employs the best cook in the city."

Everyone except Avra nods their approval. "Are you saying that we won't get to cook, ever?" Avra asks.

Ernestine shrugs. "You won't need to, but if you want to, I don't see why you couldn't. I usually have to do all the cooking and cleaning at my house."

An unsettling idea comes to me. "Won't the cook get suspicious if she's asked to cook so much food every day?"

Ernestine shakes her head. "She's been told that six people have been hired to remodel the basement and do the landscaping. She's used to cooking for employees."

"What about you, Ernestine?"

"Cook Freda knows me. Florence and I have been friends for 14 years. Cook Freda thinks I've been hired to supervise the remodel, so I'll be eating here too."

The frown on my face doesn't budge. "I still think she might get suspicious after a while."

"She might, but that's not your concern. Florence has a way of getting people to see her point of view about things."

Avra smiles at Ernestine. "I like to make victuals. I'll cook if Florence's cook needs a break."

Ernestine turns the corners of her mouth up at Avra as she slides her empty plate away from herself. "So, the plan for today is to teach you all about life outside the complex. This meal we are eating is called breakfast, not 7:00 victuals."

Avra looks perplexed. "Really? Breffest?"

"Breakfast."

"Oh, breakfast."

"Yes. The next meal we eat is called lunch. The last meal of the day is called dinner."

Rocky's blank eyes reveal that he is still slightly under the influence of the complex's medication. "When do we eat lunch, Mother?"

"Call me, Mom, son. Sometime between noon and one o'clock usually, but today it will be later."

Rocky scrunches up his eyebrows. "So lunch is really noon victuals."

Ernestine rolls her eyes in exasperation. "I don't want you to call them that anymore. Out here, only cowboys say victuals, and you are far from a cowboy."

Scott slaps the table in amazement. "Boy cows talk?"

My mother joins us again to clear the table. She chuckles as she sees the wonder on Scott's face. Ernestine almost hides her

17

low laugh with a cough. "No. People who herd cows are called cowboys."

Scott is embarrassed. "Of course. Sorry, Ernestine. Keep going."

"Don't be embarrassed. This will all make sense to you soon enough. The tops you boys are wearing are called shirts. The bottoms are called pants."

We all nod nervously. I've read about these things before, but it's hard to remember it all. Maybe I should get a piece of paper and pencil to take notes. Avra looks like she's overwhelmed to the point of tears.

Ernestine looks at Avra sideways and pats her hand. "What's the matter, Avra?"

"Mentor Ernestine, will you help me find my parents?" Avra asks sincerely.

"Yes, I will, child. But you cannot call me Mentor. It's just Ernestine. Got it?"

"Yes, M-Ernestine."

"We will start looking for parents as soon as the security guards stop scouring the city and these two have healed up." Ernestine points to Garth and me with two outstretched fingers. We hear clamoring coming from the stairway. I turn as a deep voice says, "Elira!" A middle-aged man in a white lab coat with balding light-brown hair rushes down the stairs with outstretched arms. I recognize him from the picture in my room. I stand up cautiously on my throbbing foot and hug him.

I wish I felt as much happiness as he obviously does, but this is my first time hugging a man, and it feels awkward to me.

I smile nervously at him as he pulls back to look at me. "Father?"

"Yes, I am your father, your dad, your daddy, Elira. I am so happy to have you back." He hugs me again and accidentally steps on my foot.

"Ahh! Ow! Gah!"

My father looks mortified. "I'm so sorry! Your mother called me at my hotel and told me you successfully escaped, but you broke toes in the process. I have everything I need to fix you up in my office. Why don't we fix those right now?"

I take a few deep breaths to stop myself from fixating on my toes. "Okay, that would be great. Can Garth come with me? He needs his ear fixed too."

My father looks at Garth's bandaged ear and then at me. "I don't want to share you quite yet. Is it okay if I send for him after your toes are taken care of?"

I look at Garth and shrug, wishing he could come with me, but I need to 'meet my father' sooner or later. I guess that will happen now. Garth smiles and motions with his hand to go with my dad. "Okay, Father. Let's go."

Chapter 3

A RICH CINNAMON SPICE AROMA fills the air as I limp up the stairs, hanging on my father's arm, to the main part of my parents' house. My mother is waiting for us at the top of the stairs. My hungry eyes take in the fine furnishings around me. "Are you, or I guess your cooks, baking something up here? It smells delicious."

"No, that is just the air freshener we use," my mother says as she takes my other arm, to ease the pressure on my toes.

"Oh, I don't know what that is."

My mother bites her lower lip. "I'll show it to you later, my dear."

As we shuffle into my father's office, I see a wall covered floor to ceiling with books, a big beautiful wooden desk, a shiny, metal push cart covered in medical instruments, and a flat, narrow bed covered in a white sheet.

"Hop onto the examination table, and I'll take a look at your toes."

I'm pretty sure he means the narrow bed thing, so I use my good foot to hoist myself onto it as I'm asked. I feel a stab of pain followed by relief as my father removes my fancy shoe. I curl my head up, off the pillow, to see both of my parents examining my toes. They talk back and forth quietly as they touch them. "See, Florence. All four of the smaller phalanges have separated from the metatarsals."

I try not to flinch when the pain flares. My father looks at me and smiles, "Elira, I am going to splint your toes and fit a stiff boot on this foot. You'll have to wear the boot for six weeks. It takes that long to heal broken bones. Since you are my flesh and blood, I would normally send you to a specialist, but a specialist would turn you in to the authorities, so this will have to do."

My mother walks to my side and takes my hand. "Focus on my face while Daddy works."

I bite the inside of my cheek in pain. "O—kay."

She smooths back my hair. "I am excited to show you the

makeup I have purchased for you. It is flesh colored, and if we apply it to your birthmark, no one will see it, unless they look very closely."

My insecurities come flooding back. "Are you ashamed of my face?"

My mother looks hurt. "No! Absolutely not. I just want you to be able to go outside and talk to people without them knowing you escaped from the Complex of Undesirables."

I hope that's true. "I—I'll try it. Do you want me to wear it around the house too?"

Her eyes melt with concern for me. "That is completely up to you, Elira. Do what makes you feel comfortable."

I think she means it. I want to be me, like I always have, but it's hard not to compare myself to the beautiful person standing before me. "Okay. Thank you for doing so much for me and my friends."

My mother brushes my hair behind my ear. Her fingers linger momentarily on my birthmark. "You are our only daughter. We would do far more if we had to."

Wait a minute. "I'm your only daughter. Do you have a son?"

My mother's eyes look down as she smooths the sleeve of my dress. "Yes. You have two older brothers who live on their own now. Greggory is attending the University of Tolsa which is an hour away from Herrington. Brock is married and has a little daughter of his own. He is the mayor of Adanlay, which is

23

five hours away from Herrington. We will let them know about your escape today. I'm sure they'll want to see you..."

My heart beats faster. I have brothers! That is amazing. "Mother, I would like to see pictures of them."

"You don't have to call me 'Mother' all the time. You can call me 'Mom' if you like. Your brothers do. I will show you some pictures of them when your toes are done."

"Oh, good! Thank you—Mom."

My father attaches the last velcro strip, as he calls it, to my big black boot and helps me sit up. "Your toes are as secure as they can be for now. Before you run back to your friends, will you tell your old man what life was like in the complex?"

I look into his longing eyes and nod. "Yes, of course."

My mother helps me get off the bed. "Why don't we sit somewhere more comfortable while you tell us your story, darling?"

"Okay."

Mother takes my arm and leads me to a room with big windows covered by white blinds, a beautiful white couch and chairs, and a big black thing with a bench and an open top. Papers covered in lines and dots are scattered all over the couch. I wonder if it's a secret code or language that I haven't learned.

She appears embarrassed as she gathers the paper clutter. "Sorry, I left my piano music all over the place last night after I was done practicing. I was so excited to get the basement ready for you that I forgot to finish cleaning up in here."

"So, you don't do the cooking, but you do the cleaning?"

I can't tell if my mother is embarrassed or something else. "Oh, no. Well, not usually. I usually have an upstairs and a downstairs housekeeper. I dismissed my downstairs housekeeper yesterday and arranged for the upstairs housekeeper to only come when everyone is asleep. I want as few people to know about you and your friends as possible. My upstairs housekeeper has been told not to go into the basement and not to touch my piano music unless I tell her to."

I nod my head as I look at the papers in her hands. "I don't know what a piano or a music is, but I can't wait to learn about it. Actually, I think I remember reading those words in a book once."

My mother shakes her head and wipes something from under her eye with a finger. "I'll teach you all about music, darling. It's a big part of my life and I hope it will become a big part of yours too. Well, that's enough about us, we want to learn everything about you. What was the complex like? Were they cruel to you?"

I open my mouth, but nothing comes out for a minute. The memories I have of the last 14 years feel like a dream already. I force my thoughts to form words. "I wish I knew how to explain it. I wasn't beaten or anything, but I was taught not to ask questions or expect affection. I lived with girls my age, we wore buttons colored according to our deformities, we were told that we were lucky to have a spot in the complex, away from the toxic world where people die every day..."

"What an absurd lie," my father exclaims.

"I didn't know it was a lie until a month ago. I had no reason to doubt my mentors."

"That breaks my heart," my mother moans.

I tell my parents everything. I tell them that the boys, through the glass, got me thinking about the inconsistencies in my world. I tell them that Mentor Maxine was the only kind mentor I had, that she let me ask questions, and helped me plan my escape.

My mother tears up for the fifth time. "I will have to look up this Maxine. I hope she wasn't punished for her part in your escape. I will reward her for helping bring my baby girl back to me."

I nod in approval. "She deserves a reward. She is the best adult I have ever known—until now."

My mother stands up and walks behind the couch to braid my hair as I finish telling my story. I think she wants to hide the reaction my words are causing. When I can't think of anything else to say about life in the complex, I stand up carefully and shuffle to look in the mirror on the wall. I don't even recognize myself, except for my half raccoon mask birthmark. The beautiful dress and fancily-braided hair make me look like a different person.

My parents follow me to the mirror and wrap their arms

around me. It feels weird, but good. I think I can get used to all this personal contact. That reminds me of my friends in the basement who are not being hugged several times a day.

I blush as I ask, "Can I hold Garth's hand when his ear is stitched up?"

My parents look at each other before my father says, "Y-yes. You can. Is this boy special to you?"

I turn away so Father can't see my face. "Yeah, he is. I owe him my life."

"You better tell me that story as well."

"Heh. heh. You probably won't like it."

My mom puts her hand on my dad's arm. "You won't like it, Ross. I heard it all from Ernestine and Rocky this morning and I am still trying to keep my composure every time I look at our girl. We better sit down."

So we sit down and I tell my father and mother how we escaped. I tell them about the laundry and garbage chutes, Mentor Briggs, the guards shooting Garth's ear off, how Garth carried me when I couldn't run with my broken toes, everything.

My father squeezes my hand. "You were so brave, Elira. All of your friends owe you their lives."

"No. I owe Garth mine."

My father leans forward and actually kisses my forehead. I feel myself twitch slightly. I hope he doesn't notice. That felt weird.

"I will do my best to fix him up. You say his fingers are stuck together... I wonder if they can be surgically separated. It is a new and uncommon procedure. The government doesn't want such a deformity to be duplicated, so they are all sent to the complex, but I wonder if Garth would be willing to try it."

"I will go get Garth," my mother says.

When she leaves, my father takes my face in his hands and looks into my eyes. "You have my eyes and my hair. You have grown into such a beautiful young woman. I'm so relieved that you weren't one of the unfortunate ones buried on the hill."

I flinch at the image his words create in my head. "There is a hill that they bury us on?" Why didn't Mentor Maxine tell me about that? "How many of us were buried on the hill?"

My father's face droops. "At least one every other day, I'd say. I know a man who works on the burying committee."

"Is the complex I came from the only complex?"

"No. I'm afraid not. There is a complex in every major city. No one in the United Cities lives more than three hours from a complex."

"Are the complexes Alexander Prystine's idea?"

My father does a double take. "How do you know the President of the United Cities' name?"

"I asked Mentor Bridget who the mentors' leader was once."

"Oh. Yes, he is the leader of the country. He didn't start the complex system, but he certainly made it worse."

"How did he make it worse?"

"The complex system has been in place for 150 years. They used to only take people with severe deformities away. Once all of the adult deformities were gone from society, they required all children to be inspected the January after they turned two. After 50 years they decided to take children with lesser deformities away to start a work house to produce cheap goods for everyone else. Alexander Prystine took office 40 years ago and decided that unsightly blemishes like yours qualified as a deformity and needed to be removed from our society. He claimed we needed to preserve the natural beauty of the people."

"So if I had been born before Prystine became president, I wouldn't have been sent to the complex?"

"That is correct. I wish I could give that man a piece of my mind."

"Avra, Garth, and Rocky still would have gone to the complex before Prystine."

"Yes. Skin abnormalities are obviously only skin deep. You were sent away because it would make Prystine uncomfortable to look at you."

I feel my blood start to boil. "What if the next President takes it a step further and locks away anyone that doesn't have a pretty enough face? Or long enough legs to be 'normal'?"

"I know our history and I'm not a fool. It could happen, Elira."

"When will Alexander Prystine stop being president?"

"When he turns 80 years old. That is another part of the complex law that many disagree with. Once a citizen turns 80 they are sent to a Complex for the Elderly. The President of the United Cities gets to keep his office until then."

"Why do they send the elderly away?"

"Elderly people display the same kind of uncomfortable problems that deformed children do. They lose function of their body parts, they lose their memory, and their speech, and they are unsightly to look at."

"So they are locked away so no one will have to look at them in their compromised state."

"Yes."

"Do you agree with that, Father?"

"No. Absolutely not. I have had many 80-year-old patients who were healthy and fully functional when they were forced into to the Complex for the Elderly. No one lasts longer than five years in there. They aren't fed well or treated with dignity. They wither away and die. My friend buries them on the hill too."

Chapter 4

I HAVE A LUMP IN MY THROAT as Garth comes in with my mother. He smiles at me and says, "I like your hair like that, Elira. You look amazing." I feel my cheeks turn red as his eyes remain on me. "I guess it's my turn to get fixed up. I hope I turn out as stunning as you." I smile shyly back at him and follow my parents and Garth to my father's office. I lean against my father's desk, glad to be distracted from the harsh realities the real world presents. *Ring*! "Ahh!" I scream as the desk vibrates beneath me. Mother pats my arm as she picks up a telephone on the desk. It looks like the one in the glass dorm, except it is tan colored. I look around the desk to see if there can possibly be someone on the other end. There isn't anyone. So who is Mother talking to?

"Okay, then. See you Friday. Bye." Mother hangs up the phone. "My friend is meeting me for lunch on Friday. Sorry to interrupt. Let's get Garth's ear stitched."

My mother changes the sheet before Garth climbs up onto the bed. He looks warily at the instruments on the metal rolling cart. He leans toward me, and I feel his breath on my cheek as he asks, "Will you hold my hand through this?"

I look into his crystal-blue eyes and grin. How can I say no to that face? The corners of my mouth turn up. "Yes, I will." We continue to look into each other's eyes as my father examines his ear and his fingers. Garth doesn't scream or flinch as he is stitched up. His ear is going to look lobe-less. It will be obvious that he is an escapee of the complex, just like me.

My father clears his throat. "I had some artificial... body parts made up for this very occasion."

I am completely shocked to hear that. "What? How can such things exist?"

"Ernestine said Rocky would need an ear to disguise himself, so I had a friend who makes dolls and mannequins put together a box of spare parts for me."

"Won't he get suspicious of something like that?"

"I got the parts a couple of months ago. I told him I was making models of human bodies for classes I teach."

"Oh."

"I have an artificial ear lobe that we can stick onto your ear so that you can go outside, Garth."

He forces his eyes away from me and says, "That would be wonderful, Doctor Hamble. Thank you." Garth turns his head right back to me. My father clicks his tongue. I think we're making him uncomfortable.

My father clears his throat. "Ahem. If you are interested, I would like to tell you about a new surgery I could do to separate your fingers. I haven't actually done it, but I've read about it and I think I could do it here."

Garth looks at his deformed hand for a few seconds before answering. "I—I'm thrilled that such a procedure exists but," he looks at his hand again like it's an old friend. "I will have to think about it. I know my hand is messed up, but it is still a part of me."

My father nods. "I understand, young man. Take all the time you need. You two need some rest so you can heal." Father takes a bottle of pills off his desk. "Take these pain pills to help you sleep."

We both obediently take the pills my father hands us. My mother pours us glasses of water from a pitcher to wash them down.

Mother slides in between Garth and me. "Elira, I will take you to your brothers' rooms, so you can see pictures of them. Garth, you can come too." That last part sounds less enthusiastic to me.

I walk a bit awkwardly in my boot, but I am thankful to be walking at all after last night. Mother leads us to my brothers' rooms down the hall. They both look so much like me, except older and no purple raccoon eye. I try not to let jealousy overtake me as I see pictures of my brothers and my parents smiling, laughing, and doing interesting things together. They are surrounded by water in one photo. I've never seen so much water in one place. It looks bright and magical. If I had not been forced into the complex, I would be in these pictures too.

"I—I think I'm ready to lie down, is that okay, Moth—Mom?"

"Of course, darling. I will tell the cook to delay lunch an hour so you can rest."

"Thank you, but what is lunch again?"

Mother's hand immediately covers her mouth. She drops it as soon as she realizes that I'm embarrassed. "It is the noon time meal. I forget that you..."

I wish she wouldn't react to my naivety so extremely, it makes me feel pathetic. "Oh, yeah. I remember now. I will catch on to all your phrases soon."

Garth tries to help me out. "Madam Hamble, I will take Elira down the stairs, so you can talk to the cook. Thank you for your hospitality."

Mother smiles at him. "Call me, Mrs. Hamble, Garth.

Thank you for your help. Please be careful with my little girl."
Her eyes say more than her words do.

"I will, Mrs. Hamble." Garth says with all seriousness. My
mother walks away looking less sure of that than he does.

I lean heavily on him as we descend the staircase. "I should
have been in those pictures, Garth."

"I know. I wish you were in those pictures too. But we can
make new memories and take new pictures now."

You know, he's right. We can't erase the past, but we can
make the future great. "You're right, I just want to break the
whole complex down. I'm not the only one being left out of
family pictures."

Garth squeezes my hand. "One day at a time. First you
heal. Then we find my parents and Avra and Scott's parents.
Once we've done that, we can talk about taking down the
complex."

A yawn escapes my mouth. "That sounds good. I should
slee—heal." When we enter the basement sitting room, our
own faces greet us on the, I believe it is called a television,
screen. That startles me to full awareness.

Jefrey stands up and scowls as he points to the screen.
"They are looking for us, Garth."

The announcer calls out our names one by one as a close
up of our faces fills the screen. "If any of you have seen these
six escapees, or their supposed accomplice, Ernestine Moore,

you are urged by penalty of law to let the authorities know immediately." The silence that fills the room is deafening.

Chapter 5

WHEN I WAKE UP FROM MY NAP, I am incredibly hungry. Avra pulls me out of bed. "Everyone is waiting for you, Elira. Let's go eat our vic—lunch." The lunch, as my mother calls it, is made of fresh delicate rolls and meats I have never tried. The fruits and vegetables provided are strange but delicious too. Ernestine eats without slowing down. It makes me feel like I can have second helpings without getting in trouble. I take a second sandwich looking warily at the adults as I do so. They don't seem to mind at all. My stomach is full for the first time in weeks.

Avra stabs an orange square of fruit on her fork. "What is this, Ernestine?"

"It's called cantaloupe."

Avra bites her piece of cantaloupe in half. "Mmm. It's good. Does it grow on trees like apples?"

Ernestine rubs her chin in frustration. "No, it grows on a plant on the ground, I think."

Scott nods his head energetically. "Yes. It does."

I turn to Scott, surprised. "How do you know that?"

"I was studying to be a gardener."

I think about how much time Scott spent communicating with Avra at the complex. "Uh, you couldn't have had much time to learn about plants before we escaped."

"I'm a year older than the rest of you. I spent the year before I met Avra studying plants so I could grow food for the complex." Oh, that's why Scott isn't as close to the rest of the boys in our gang.

Ernestine swallows loudly. "Speaking of that horrible work-house, the officer on the news today said that they think someone on the inside of the complex helped you out."

My heart drops. "Do they know it was Maxine?"

"No, not yet, but they will probably figure it out."

My happy stomach decides to start twisting into a knot. "I feel so bad. I wish I could help her."

"The best thing you can do is stay put and get healed up." Ernestine takes another big bite of sandwich and swallows. "I wish we knew what you three's last names are. I can look up addresses if I have a last name."

Avra shakes her head. "I don't know my last name. I've always been Avra 286."

"Huh. What does the number represent?" Ernestine asks.

Avra frowns. "I don't know."

I have an idea. "I don't know for sure, but I think we're numbered as we're placed into the complex."

Mother chimes in, "I believe so. My husband has asked his colleagues who work at the complex in the past. Once the number reaches 9999, they start over again at 1. The lifespan for... residents of the complex is not very long, and they don't want to keep track of five-digit numbers."

"Don't look so sad, kids. You're out now. I can ask around to see if anyone knows of a couple who lost twin boys to the complex. That is a pretty rare occurrence. You two, your parents will be a little bit harder to track down," Ernestine says as she jabs her fork at Avra and Scott. Scott reaches for Avra's hand.

My mother sets her knife and fork down in a prim and dainty way. "Ernestine, don't get their hopes up. Not all parents are like us. Some people have been severely indoctrinated by the government's propaganda. This could all end in tears."

Jefrey jumps into the conversation, "I agree. I think we'll get caught if we go looking for our parents. It's not safe. We better not."

Avra's face wilts before my eyes. I wish Jefrey would think twice before speaking. I tilt my head toward Avra and mouth the words 'shut up' to him. He rolls his eyes at me.

Ernestine looks at Jefrey and Florence. "Have a little faith in me. I will watch the parents for a long time. I'll get the feel for what they're like before I risk taking the kids there."

My mother looks intently at her less-elegant friend. "I sincerely hope so."

We 'kids' sit quietly, eating our lunch as the adults talk over us. I really don't want Avra's weak heart to be broken by parents who were glad to be rid of her. I can't imagine that she has one of the few horrible sets of parents out there, though. Right?

We all help clean up lunch in silence. I glare at Jefrey one more time when I see a tear trickle down Avra's cheek. Ernestine reassures us that things will work out and directs us to the comfortable sofas and chairs in the common room, or great room, as my mother calls it. Jefrey taps me on the shoulder and asks me if he can have a word with me. I nod, and hobble to the corner with him.

Jefrey's blue eyes are dark and keep darting around. "It seems like you have given up on me, Elira."

I can tell he feels hurt which makes me feel bad, but I think we should be honest with each other. "You've made it clear that you did not want to escape and wish we were still back there. I feel so differently that I don't know if we can ever..."

Jefrey's eyes burn into mine. "I'm stuck in this new life with you. Can't you give me another chance?"

Is that really the word he just used? "Stuck, huh?"

"Sorry, that's not what I meant to say."

"What did you mean to say?"

"Come sit by me at the table so we can have more privacy," Jefrey whispers as he takes my hand and leads me to the table. I'm trying to decide how his hand feels on my own. Garth turns his head to watch our progress, then gets off the couch and walks into the boys' room and shuts the door.

Avra raises her eyebrows at me as she squeezes Scott's hand from the sofa. I turn away from everyone and try to act interested in a painting on the wall.

Jefrey tries to get me to look at him. "Elira, I used to know what each day would be like in the complex. I had a routine and I liked it. Now, I am constantly looking over my shoulder. I feel like the authorities are right outside the door and will take us back any minute now."

I look at him and try to understand how hard it must be to miss routine and to fear the unknown. I feel like my whole life has been filled with unknowns. This isn't any different. I just have parents and friends who will answer my questions and help me know what is going on. "Jefrey, do you trust my parents and Ernestine?"

"Y-yes. I guess so."

"Do you think they want to help you?"

41

He shrugs his shoulders. "Yeah. It seems like it."

"I can promise you that they care more about you than any of your mentors did. We can study and become whatever we want to out here."

"I could do that in the complex too."

"No, you couldn't. You were lucky to be a yellow, but you had 12 choices only. Once you became too sick to put in seven days a week of hard labor they would kill you. My dad knows someone who buries a body every other day from the complex." Jefrey shakes his head like he doesn't trust me. "I can't believe you still believe that the complex was there to help you. It was there to use you."

"The complex may have had some secret plans, but I never felt used."

"I'll have my mother take you to buy cheap goods that our friends made for no pay. If reality hasn't sunk in by then, I don't know if it ever will."

I try to stand up, but he grabs my hand so I'll stay put. "I hear what you're saying, but it is going to take time for me to understand this new world. Will you help me? Elira, please?"

I wish his face didn't look so handsome or so pitiful. "Yes, Jefrey. I'll help you. We will figure out this new world together."

"Thank you."

"That's what friends do."

Ernestine brings out a long, thin box and sets it on the little table in front of the sofa. I want to know what is in the box, so I stand up and walk over to her. Jefrey follows me and sits by me on the couch.

"Rocky, I want to teach you how to play chess. Your— uh— father and I used to play it all the time. It teaches you to think ahead before making a move. That will be an important skill to master as fugitives and you're going to need something to do when you are stuck down here. The rest of you kids listen in. We have an hour or two before Florence comes back from the store."

Scott walks to the boys' bedroom door and sticks his head in for a few seconds. Garth walks out of their bedroom, gives me half a smile and sits down across the room from me. I smile at him, but I can tell he's not happy that I'm sitting by Jefrey. Ernestine starts explaining what each piece of the game does and I'm grateful for the distraction from Jefrey's longing gaze. I easily memorize how each piece on the board moves. Rocky places his pieces in safe spots at first, but as the game progresses, I keep warning him not to move his pieces in danger's way.

"Sometimes you have to sacrifice a piece in order to win, Elira," Ernestine tells me as I'm about to warn Rocky again.

"That doesn't really make sense," Jefrey says.

"I'll play you next, Jefrey, so you can understand."

"No. I don't want to play. I'll just watch."

"Fine. Suit yourself."

Rocky loses to his mother after a long, overly-merciful

game and then challenges me. "If you're so smart, see if you can beat me."

I sit tall on the edge of my seat. "Oh, I will." Avra giggles at me as she leans forward to watch.

Maybe I shouldn't have spoken so soon. I was sure I was going to win because I took more of Rocky's pieces than he took of mine, but just like his mom warned me, he sacrificed an important piece, his queen, to win the game. I didn't see his rook because I was so focused on the queen. Rocky smiles at me as he tips my king over. "Checkmate, game over. Nice try."

I frown in disappointment. How did I let myself get distracted from what really mattered? I need to think about this before I play again. Ernestine smiles at me. "Do you want a rematch, Elira?"

"Yes, but tomorrow." *Thud*. I whip my head around to see what's going on in the kitchen.

Mother places a big box on the table. Garth is immediately by my side. He takes my hand and helps me hobble to the kitchen. Jefrey glares at us the whole way. I feel like I am doing something wrong by him. What should I do? I don't want life to be hostile and uncomfortable here. Ahh.

My mother smiles with delight as we gather around the table. "I have disguises for you all. Let's see how different we can make you, so you can go outside soon." I look into the box with curiosity. There is hair dye of every color, fake noses and ears, makeup, earrings, sunglasses, sideburns, and eyebrows. I want to reach in and grab something, but I have no idea what I should try.

Ernestine picks up a fake nose and turns to my mother. "I hope you didn't buy all of this at a single store today. With the breakout all over the news, someone will turn you in for suspicious behavior for sure."

"I only bought some of the hair dye today. I've had most of this stuff for years. I knew we'd get our kids out someday and we'd have to disguise them." Mother holds up a bottle of blonde hair dye. "I always have this on hand to cover up my gray roots."

Ernestine throws the fake nose back in the box. "You amaze me, sometimes, Florence."

My mother smiles at her friend and starts playing with the end of my braid. "Elira, I think we should cut your hair short and dye it blonde. What do you think?"

I look at the bottle of blonde hair dye my mother is extending toward me. I've never had the option to change my hair color. "I, uh, sure, if you think so, Mother."

"I think that blonde will look the most different yet natural with your features." She sets the hair dye on the table and picks up another little bottle. "Here is the flesh colored makeup I was telling you about."

"Okay, I'll try it. How short should I cut my hair?"

"A pixie cut would look adorable on you."

"Okay, I don't know what that is, but, if you think so."

Mother turns to my best friend and starts picking through

her thinning hair. "Avra, I don't think dyeing your black hair will look natural, but many girls with your coloring do caramel-colored streaks in their hair. What do you think? Or, maybe I can find some caramel-colored hair extensions to fill in the thinning parts of your hair more."

Avra looks at my mother with appreciation. "Yes. I would love that, thank you."

A giggle escapes my mother's lips when she sees Garth wearing a bushy black mustache. "You boys need to decide on a color to dye your hair. Garth and Jefrey, we don't want you to look like twins anymore, so pick different hair colors." The twins look at each other with uncertainty as that news sinks in. "Garth, there is an artificial earlobe you can stick on. As long as someone doesn't stare at it in close proximity, no one will know it's fake."

Garth picks up a flesh-colored half moon and squishes it with his fingers. "Thank you."

Jefrey picks a bottle out of the box. "I will go black. Garth, pick something else."

Garth looks at his brother with annoyance. He looks at the remaining colors of dye and chooses one. "I will go with this then." Mother looks at his choice and nods her approval. "What color would you call this, Mrs. Hamble?"

"I'd just call it reddish-brown."

Knock, knock. Did someone just knock at the outside door? I'm pretty sure guests for Doctor and Mrs. Hamble come to the door upstairs by the piano room, not the concrete-encased basement door. I look at the basement windows and am relieved that the blinds are shut tight with no gaps.

Ernestine jumps out of her kitchen chair and starts throwing bottles in the box. "It might be peace officers. We have to hide all of this and ourselves, now!" We grab everything off the table and run for the bookshelf. I pull the red book out and jerk the hidden door open. We all pile into the room with our arms full and shut the door.

My heart is racing and I'm afraid my breathing will be audible through the bookshelf. I close my eyes and hold my breath for 10 seconds to calm myself down. When I open my eyes, I notice Avra looking wobbly. I gesture to Scott to help her sit on the couch. He helps her sit down, sidles up next to her, and puts his arm around her shoulders. I suddenly hear a loud, deep male voice talking to Florence, or I should say— Mom. I press my ear to the door to hear everything better. Rocky and Ernestine join me.

"...Mrs. Hamble. Sorry for the back-door approach, I've just been patrolling your street, and I wondered if you've had any strange people loitering on your property. I'm sure you've seen the news. Some undesirables escaped from the complex, and we have reason to believe they are hiding somewhere in town."

I look nervously at Garth, who has joined me at the door.

He takes my hand. Jefrey glares at him as he butts into our space.

"Thank you so much for your concern, officer. I keep a highly vigilant staff, and they have not seen anyone loitering around here at all, but we will keep a tighter lookout."

"One of the escaped undesirables is your daughter."

"Really? I was sure she was dead by now."

"No. She is not dead."

"With a blotched face like hers, she'll be turned in by today, I'm sure." My stomach drops. She's only pretending my face is repulsive, right?

"Hmm. Do you always sit in the basement alone, Mrs. Hamble?"

"I do quite often, yes. I'm forming a plan to redecorate the basement, so I'm sitting down here to imagine the possibilities."

"Do you mind if I look around?"

"By all means, officer."

The peace officer sounds like he is opening and shutting all of the closets and cupboards in the great room. I wonder what he will do when he sees that the bedrooms look lived in.

The officer's voice is ridiculously loud in general but it gets harder to make out as he explores the far corners of the basement. I press my ear hard against the door. "This bedroom appears to be occupied. Who is staying in it?"

Avra starts rocking back and forth on the sofa next to

Scott. He takes her hand and guides her head to his shoulder so she doesn't make any noise.

"All of the basement bedrooms are being occupied at the moment. I've hired a crew of six to help me redecorate the basement and to update my landscaping."

"They are staying in the same rooms you want redecorated…"

"It's the great room that I want to redecorate."

"Where are these workers now?"

"They went to the hardware store to buy paint and supplies."

"You don't say."

"They'll start taping off the ceiling and trim when they get back."

"It looks like your deformed daughter's room is pretty exquisite."

I cringe, thinking of the nightgown I left on the floor, and the unmade bed…

"It's basically a second guest room. I really should tear all that old garbage off the walls and repaint."

"Which would explain why the hired help is staying in there…"

Mother doesn't miss a beat. "I'm just imagining the possibilities now. Pictures of that unsightly blemish turns my stomach. I really should redecorate this room. Thank you for the idea. Would you like to pop up to the kitchen for some lemon cake on your way out? My cook's lemon cake is legendary."

"I-uh, don't mind if I do. Thank you, Mrs. Hamble."

Avra releases her death grip on Scott. I step away from the door and start pacing. We have been lazy, and foolish. I use a loud whisper to say, "We can't leave any evidence of who we are laying around our bedrooms. We should probably put all of our personal belongings in here."

Rocky whispers back, "It's not like we have any personal belongings. We should destroy our jumpsuits though."

"I'm pretty sure my mom already did."

Jefrey stops my pacing and gets right in my face. "So much for a safe place, Elira. Why is living like this better than the complex, again? Remind me. I'm not sure I'm seeing it."

I can't come up with a smart remark fast enough. "I'm sure the officer is leaving soon, so calm down."

He throws his arms out at the room. "This locked room is smaller than the locked dorm in the complex. This is like a prison."

Garth slams Jefrey in the chest. "Get out of her face, Jef. We are better off, and you know it."

Avra's quiet voice chimes in, "They were going to kill me soon. I'm glad we're out."

Ernestine puts a calming hand on Jefrey's arm. "I'm sure every house in the city is being searched right now. It won't always be this way."

Click. The door opens and my mother walks in. She can see the tension on our faces. "It's okay, he's gone. The officer looked around but didn't find anything besides your pajamas on the ground." We all breathe a sigh of relief. "We should keep any belongings that reveal who you are hidden in here, but don't be too worried. I think he believed my story."

Jefrey pushes past my mother and storms out. Ernestine looks at my mother and me and holds up a pair of scissors. "Let's get these kids disguised right now, just in case."

Chapter 6

I LOOK AT MYSELF IN THE MIRROR. I can't believe the person's face I'm seeing is really mine. My dress is so beautiful, my hair is short, and it's blonde like my mothers. But more importantly, my scar has disappeared. The makeup my mother gave me worked incredibly well. The skin of my birthmark is still a bit raised, but you have to look closely to see it. I hope my mother will like seeing my face without my 'unsightly blemish.'

Avra joins me at the mirror. Her hair is short and 'cut in a trendy way' according to my mom. The caramel streaks are fancy. She looks like she belongs in my mother's world, for sure. I turn around and look at the boys. Scott has attached fake hair extensions and braided it all into what Ernestine calls cornrows and is wearing a big, fake nose. His lumpy neck is completely covered with a high-necked shirt called a turtle neck. I wouldn't know it was him if I were a complex mentor. Rocky bleached his hair blonde. He has a fake ear glued on, a fake little blonde beard thing called a goatee and green-colored eye coverings called contacts. Garth looks different but still amazing with spikey reddish-brown hair, long fake side burns, and brown contacts. Jefrey looks as dark and sharp as he acts with black-colored contacts, hair, and eyebrows. He has just a sliver of fake black hair on his chin.

Ernestine looks at us and nods. "That's what I'm talking about." She has seven less inches of dark curly hair on her head and a fake chin on that protrudes much farther than her real one. "We'll spend the rest of the day working on your vocabulary. If your looks don't give you away, your speech might."

Avra likes what she sees in the mirror. "When will we be able to go outside?"

"If you can master the vocabulary changes I teach you today, I think we could try a short test trip to the convenience store tomorrow. What do you think, Florence?"

"There are peace officers everywhere. They definitely

couldn't all go together. A group of six is dangerous with six faces on the news right now."

"Okay. We'll send groups of two or three to the convenience store in the morning and the afternoon tomorrow to see if they can pass as normal citizens, if and only if they take my vocabulary lessons seriously."

Avra and Scott smile nervously at each other. I take Garth aside and whisper in his ear, "Will you go with me?"

He moves some of my short blonde hair behind my ear. "Absolutely."

Jefrey guesses what we're talking about and joins us. "You two aren't going anywhere without me." Just great.

When Ernestine calls us all in for vocabulary lessons, Jefrey beckons me to sit next to him on the—loveseat, as my mom calls it. I pretend like I don't see him and sit on the couch next to Rocky and Garth. If anyone is going to master the real-world vocabulary, it's going to be me. I want to go outside in the sunshine and feel the wind blowing my hair, and I kind of wonder what it will be like to meet new people who don't immediately look at my raccoon eye.

Ernestine clears her throat to command our attention. "Repeat after me: I eat breakfast in the morning, lunch at noon, and dinner in the evening. My favorite place to eat is a restaurant called 'Ollie's' and I get my hair done at Shannon's Salon."

We all take our real-world lessons seriously. Of course, we

want to go outside. Ernestine is finally smiling at our answers to her questions by 10:30 pm. She says we're ready for tomorrow morning. I'll be counting down the minutes until breakfast.

AS SCOTT AND I WASH the breakfast dishes, I giggle at how wrinkly my fingers get. Maybe I should disguise myself as an elderly person. Ernestine puts the last coat of glue on her fake jaw. "I say we try this out. I'm going to take Rocky and Scott to the convenience store and see if anyone recognizes us."

Florence shakes her head. "No, you two are number one and two on the wanted list. Let's start this believability test on the safe side. I'll take Elira and Garth instead."

"Oh no, not without me," Jefrey butts in.

I roll my eyes at him. The constant jealousy permeating this basement is ruining my time with both twins.

Mother is soon persuaded. "Okay, Jefrey, you can come too. We need to see if people can tell that you're twins still." She digs through her shoulder bag thing that I vaguely remember is called a purse and pulls out a rectangular envelope that she extends toward the twins. "Take this money. We'll walk to the little store down the street and buy a bag of chips."

We all look at each other blankly. Garth clears his throat. "I'm not sure if I can tell the difference between a house and store yet, Mrs. Florence."

My mother lets out a long breath. "Just Florence or Mrs. Hamble. I'm sorry. I forget that you don't... Ernestine, are you sure they're ready?"

"Yes. They are. They'll be fine for a 20-minute trip."

"You're probably right, but only because I convinced the peace officer yesterday that I was disgusted that my blemished daughter escaped the complex. He said he was shorthanded for the amount of surveillance that is being asked of him. I convinced him that we didn't need to be under 24-hour-a-day-observation. Who knows how long we can go unwatched. Anyway, I will go with you to the convenience store, but I can't go inside with you. It'll seem odd if I go to the convenience store with my hired help. But I think we should give you all a lesson on using money first."

Ernestine nods her head. "Yes. Good call. I almost forgot about that."

Jefrey looks curiously at my mother. "Why do we need money? We didn't use it in the complex."

"It takes money to pay for the things we need. Very few people trade goods or services anymore. Money is what paid for this house and the breakfast you just ate. It is necessary in this world for survival. The less money you have, the less options you have to buy what you want or need."

Jefrey shifts his head from side to side. "So the more money you have, the more you can get the stuff you want."

She nods, "In a nutshell, yes." Jefrey grins.

Mother patiently shows us the different amounts of money that each coin and bill from her purse represent. She has us pretend to buy something and figure out the correct change to get back. Jefrey lights up during this little lesson. He insists on holding the money for us.

"Don't hold the envelope in front of you like that. You're asking to get robbed. Put it in your pocket instead," Ernestine says grumpily. Jefrey shoves the envelope into the pocket of his... pants, yeah. That's what they're called.

"Yes. Just like that." Mother smiles at us all nervously and opens the door. Ready or not, here we come. She sticks her head out the door before letting us out. "I don't see any peace officers. This is a good time to go. Come on."

The air is so cold it takes my breath away. Mother hears me gasp. "Do you need a jacket, Elira? It is breezy today," She says with concern.

"No, I'm fine," I lie as the wind stings my exposed skin. My mother hands me some dark glasses that protect my eyes from the sun and cover the raised skin of my scar. I realize that my foot in a boot will be note-worthy to a society with no deformities. "Mother, my boot, won't they question that?"

"Yes, you're right. People still get hurt, but it isn't very common. Maybe you and I should sit on a bench outside while the boys go in and make the purchase."

"I thought you wanted to test our..."

Mother lowers her voice. "Don't you want to be outside, Elira? I saw you peeking out the blinds yesterday."

I feel foolish realizing she has noticed my yearning for the outdoors. "Yes, I have always wanted to spend time outside. It's surprising how cool the wind is. But I love the sun." I look up at the bright circle in the sky and smile as the warm rays fall on my pale cheeks.

"I'm tired of standing still. Let's go." Jefrey insists.

"Shut up, Jef," Garth says under his breath.

We walk as fast as I can hobble to the little glass-fronted building down the street. Mother clears her throat. "Garth do you see the difference between this building with merchandise for sale in the big windows and the building across the street with fewer, smaller windows and lots of grass?" Garth nods. "Which do you think is the house and which do you think is the store?"

"We're at the store. There isn't much grass, so vehicles can park here while the people buy things inside."

"Correct. Vehicles pull up to these machines to buy gasoline for fuel too." Garth nods as he watches a man put a hose thing into the side of his car.

Mother pats both twins on the arm. "Well, this is the moment of truth. Go in there and buy a bag of chips. Good luck!" Garth smiles nervously at us as Jefrey drags him into the store. He hides his deformed hand in the pocket of his pants.

There is a wooden bench along the side of the building.

I limp over to it and ease myself down. My mother joins me. I giggle as I watch a furry little animal scurry up a nearby tree. My mother smiles at me. "You take delight in the smallest things, Elira. It is so refreshing and charming compared to your brothers."

"What are my brothers like?"

Mother purses her lips as she gathers her thoughts. "Brock is a strong, determined man. He works hard and is already a well-liked mayor at his relatively young age. He is a bit of a social climber. He won't stop until he reaches the top."

"What's the top?"

"President of the United Cities."

I think about what my father taught me about the President of the United Cities yesterday. Ernestine told us even more during our lessons last night. The President has to be voted in and becomes the head boss of everyone until he retires to the Complex for the Elderly at age 80. Why would my own brother want to become the boss of everyone? "Does Brock approve of the complex system?"

Mother sighs. "We taught our sons not to approve of it, but we were cautious, and encouraged them to be careful when voicing their opinions as well. I think Brock will do whatever it takes to become President. Even if it means going against the way we raised him."

"I hope not. It would help so many people if the next President changed the law about the complex."

"You're right. It would."

"What about my other brother, Greggory?"

Mother sniffs. "He is the opposite of Brock. He isn't driven. He wants us to take care of him so he doesn't have to work, and what we give him is never enough. He thinks he deserves the world. He is at school now only because we told him we'd cut off all money support if he didn't go to at least a few classes a semester."

"I don't know what a semester is. When will his schooling be done?"

"As long as he passes all of his classes, one year."

"Will he come back here to live with us?"

Mother frowns. "Not if I can help it." That surprises me. My mother seems so happy to have me and my friends living with her. Why does she feel so differently about her other child?

The boys walk out of the store just then. "We did it! See, chips!" Garth exclaims as he holds up a small brown bag.

My mother chuckles to herself. "Those are chocolate chips. I meant corn or potato chips, but that's okay. Did they seem suspicious of you?"

Jefrey shakes his head. "No. The woman pointed to a stand with these bags in it and said that they received a large shipment of chocolate chips by mistake and they were selling them at cost if we wanted a good deal. We took a bag and gave her all of our money, and she gave us this much back."

Mother counts out the change. "That seems about right. It wouldn't have surprised me if she had cheated you."

Jefrey seems confused. "Why would someone do that?"

"Some people's goal is to get as much money as they can, even if they cheat others to get it. Could the woman tell you were twins?"

Jefrey shakes his head. "I don't think so. She asked if we were friends or coworkers. I said 'friends.'"

Garth walks up to me and helps me off the bench. He holds my hand as we walk back to the house. I see my mom glance at our hands every so often. I wonder if it bothers her. It doesn't bother me. My hand has never felt so alive. It's so much better than reaching through a hole in the wall. I walk as slowly as I can so this experience doesn't have to end. Jefrey walks right behind us, glaring at the backs of our heads.

When we get back to the house, we are shocked to see that Ernestine is gone. "Where is she?" my mother demands.

"She said she needs to start investigating our parents," Scott says nervously. "She has two possible addresses for my parents, and she went to check them out. She said she would be back before dark."

"She had better be."

Well, she isn't. Our hearts sink as the sun goes down. Did someone recognize her? Are the authorities on their way now? What should we do? My mother tells the rest of my friends that they will have to go to the convenience store another day. My father leaves to go look for Ernestine as the rest of us eat our dinner in silence.

Bam, bam, bam. We pick up our dishes and rush to the hidden room. When the door clicks into place, I hear my mother answer the outside door. "Ernestine! I could kill you! Were you seen?"

"No one had a clue who I was, Florence. Don't get all worked up about nothing."

"How did you know where to look?"

"I've heard rumor about a few parents who are unhappy with the complex for taking their kids. These two I checked on today have the same light brown skin tone as Scott. Florence— are you sure we should let them out before we've finished this conversation?"

"Yes. They've lived their lives believing that adults use them and hide important information from them on purpose. I don't want them to feel that way here."

Click. The hidden door swings open and we all burst out, wanting to join the conversation.

My mother gets the first word. "Ernestine, what would you like to say to Rocky, Scott, and Avra, who were so excited to go to the convenience store today?"

Ernestine looks at Mother's frowning face, then at my three anxious friends, and frowns to herself. "I'm sorry, kids. I really thought I'd be back sooner. I'll take you tomorrow instead. Well, if the peace officer sitting outside in his car is gone by then."

Mother rolls her eyes. "I knew it."

Scott, of all people, speaks up first. "Did you find my parents?"

Ernestine's face breaks out into a huge toothy smile. "Maybe. One of the dads looks a lot like you."

Scott claps his hands together excitedly. "Ha ha! What were they like?"

"Oh—I didn't get a chance to talk to them in person. I'm pretty sure they have an officer watching their house too. The authorities know who escaped, and who their parents are by now. When I watched them having a conversation with a peace officer, they seemed annoyed. If they are your parents, that's a good sign. I'm sure that means they want him to leave, so they can have you back." My mother glares at Ernestine who backpedals a little bit. "It might not be your parents though. Most people in town are annoyed by peace officer interrogations."

Scott claps his hands. "I still think that's a good sign. I can't wait to meet them."

Ernestine pulls off her fake chin. "We're getting close, Scott. Be patient."

My mother stomps her foot. "Stop encouraging this, Ernestine. We need to stay put and do our research for now.

After a few weeks, I'm sure the peace officers will tire of watching houses with nothing going on."

"But I was fine!"

"Why were you back so late then? You had a hard time dodging all the officers in town, didn't you?"

Ernestine's excitement drains from her face. "Fine, we'll do some research for a while. You kids prepare yourselves for some long, boring days."

Avra clears her throat. "I don't think finding my parents is boring."

My mother gives Avra a one-armed hug. "Of course, you don't, my dear. I'm sure we'll find all kinds of interesting information about them."

"I can't wait," she says longingly.

Ernestine yawns and tousles Rocky's bleached head. "It's been a long day, kids. Let's get some shut-eye." We all mumble our agreement.

As we move toward the bedrooms, my mother stops Garth and me in our tracks. I let go of his warm hand reluctantly as my mother links arms with him. "Garth, you need to have your ear stitches cleaned." He shoots me a cute smile before he ascends the stairs with my mother.

On the way to my room, Jefrey stops me. He is standing uncomfortably close. "Elira, do you want to practice counting money with me?"

"Actually, I..."

"Please?"

"Uh, only for a few minutes."

I walk to the table and watch Jefrey pull an envelope of money from one of the drawers in the kitchen. "Here it is."

I look at him curiously. "How did you know where the money was?"

"I watched your mom put it there."

"Oh. Give me one dollar and eighty cents."

He whips a dollar and some coins over to me in no time flat. "Am I right?"

"Yes. Good job. Your turn."

"Give me nine dollars and five cents."

I count out every dollar from the envelope which only adds up to eight and then count the coins which add up to 105 cents. "How did you know that there was exactly nine dollars and five cents in the envelope?"

Jefrey grins mischievously. "I don't know, lucky guess."

I frown at him. "Right."

"Why are you so mad at me?"

I sigh, "Why do you even like me, Jefrey?"

"You're beautiful."

"What else do you like?"

"Uh, well," he struggles to come up with something. "That dress is stunning on you."

"There's a lot more to me than my looks. I hope you have

more substance than that." I get up and go to my room despite Jefrey's protests.

Chapter 7

"AVRA, DO YOU HAVE ANY IDEA which of these things is a razor?" I ask as I open and close drawers in the bathroom the next morning.

"I have no idea."

I scratch my head. "Do you know what a razor does?"

"Nope."

"I think it has something to do with legs. My mom is ashamed of my legs. If I figure out which of these things is a razor, it will help my legs look better, I think."

Knock knock. Avra opens the door and finds my mom

standing there. "Hello, girls. I was wondering if you wanted help learning about your new clothes and hygiene products."

I wrap my robe around me tighter as I approach my beautiful mother. "I want to learn about razors."

Mother looks at my legs and barely hides her dismay. "I would be happy to help you, Elira."

Mother takes us into the bathroom and shows us what a razor and shaving cream are. I love the fluffy texture of the shaving cream and am amazed at how smooth my leg is after I glide a purple razor along it.

"Do all women take the hair off their legs out here?" Avra asks.

My mother tilts her head to the side as she thinks about that. "No, not all, but the women I associate with do."

"I like it," I say as I rub my hands up and down my legs over and over again.

Avra looks at my mom sheepishly. "Will you help me, Miss Florence?"

"Just Florence, Avra. Absolutely. Choose a different colored razor from Elira's so you don't mix them up."

Avra picks a pink razor and gets just as much delight out of the smoothness of her legs as I do.

"I would suggest shaving your legs before wearing a dress or shorts. Come into the closet and I'll show you what I'm talking about." We follow my mom into the closet and look at the dresses, skirts, and shorts of varying lengths that she shows us.

"Most women wear dresses for special occasions. The skirts and shorts are for casual occasions. These pants are casual too. Those pants over there are dress pants, so they are worn on special occasions."

My head is spinning. How am I supposed to know how dressy I'm supposed to be? "When is the next special occasion?"

My mother slowly sets the pair of high heels she's holding on the shoe shelf and sniffs. "I wish you could go to church with us each Sunday morning in a dress and have lunch with my friends every first Friday, but for now, you won't be going anywhere that requires dressy clothing."

I don't want her to be unhappy. "Can I wear a dress just for myself around the basement?"

My mother snaps out of her sad stupor. "Yes. You can wear whatever you want around the house. If you are doing a messy project, I'd rather you not wear silk though."

I smile cheerfully at my mother. "Okay. Will you help me pick out something casual that people on the outside would think is pretty?"

"Yes. Absolutely. I picked out some cute shirts for you the day Ernestine told me she was communicating with you through the complex window."

"How did Ernestine know I was your daughter?"

"Elira is not a very common name."

"You knew I'd find my way here?"

"Yes. I knew you would, darling. That shirt looks striking with those pants. I'd stick with those for today. That outfit will set the right tone in case they show up today."

My eyes narrow in on my mom. "In case who shows up today?"

Mother flips her hand like it doesn't matter. "Don't worry about it. Now, Avra, which color do you prefer? Pink or turquoise?"

She taps a finger on her chin. "I like them both, but I'll try the Tur koys."

Avra is a beautiful person. She could wear a garbage bag and still look nice. Mother smiles at my friend when she pulls on the turquoise shirt. "Both colors look stunning with your skin tone, Avra. Wear these pants with that shirt. My husband wants you to come upstairs to his office so he can listen to your heart."

Avra's eyes fill with concern. "I usually take a special medicine for my heart. I hope he can get me some."

"I'm sure he can. He can probably find you something newer and better too."

I smile as Mother braids my friend's hair and helps her decide which shoes to wear. I think they both like this accessorizing stuff.

I TAKE ROCKY'S BISHOP WITH MY ROOK and smile maliciously at him.

"Nice move," he says dejectedly.

I see Avra come down the stairs, back from seeing my dad. I pat the spot on the couch next to me. "So, what did the doctor say?"

Avra gives me a crooked grin. "He's your dad. You can call him Dad. He said that my heart is weaker than he expected, but he has a new heart medicine that he wants me to try. He says that his elderly patients have done really well on it."

"You're not elderly."

"I know, but I think the only sick people out here are elderly."

"Oh, yeah. That's weird to me, but it makes sense."

Mother rushes down the stairs. "Elira, I need you to come upstairs."

I look at the chess board in front of me. I'm close to beating Rocky for once. "Do I have to come right now?"

"Yes. You will want to meet the people who have just arrived."

What? I am so confused. I look at my mother's happy face questioningly. "I can't meet people. They'll turn me in!"

Rocky stands up. "It's okay, Elira. You can trust her. We can finish our game when you get back."

Mother takes my hand and stands me up. "These people won't turn you in." Curiosity, nerves, and my mother's hand lead me up the stairs. I hope she knows what she's doing.

I have no idea who the people staring at me are when my mother leads me into the formal sitting room. Mother lets go of my hand, puts her arm around my shoulders, and gives me a gentle squeeze instead. "Elira, these are your brothers, Brock and Greggory."

The pictures in my brothers' rooms come rushing back to me. They don't look exactly like those pictures, but I recognize our similarities now. Brock is pleasant looking with thick light-brown hair like mine, well, before it was dyed. He is dressed in a stunning black suit. His wife is short with long blonde hair that has been carefully curled into ringlets. She is wearing an incredibly fancy blue dress and seems to have a permanent scowl on her face. Their little girl is adorable though. I haven't seen a child in person since I was one myself. Mother notices my fascination and tells me, "Joy is three years old." The little girl has light-brown hair curled into ringlets like her mom. She is dressed in a purple frilly dress which, of course, I love. When she smiles at me, I can't help but smile back. Greggory, on the other hand, looks like—a slob. He could be just as handsome as Brock, but he has let his blonde hair and beard grow out in a messy, slovenly way. His shirt is not tucked into his pants, it could use a wash, and when he looks at me, I see his lips sneer.

My mother nervously introduces everyone. Brock's wife's

name is Chantilly. The look on her face shows her distaste for the room we are in, or maybe it's me. I don't understand it. I am in complete awe at the magnificence of this house. My father walks up beside me and gives me a one-armed squeeze. It's like he's trying to tell my brothers that he claims me, no matter how strange the circumstances are.

Greggory swaggers across the room to me and shakes my hand. His hand is strong yet smooth. He must not use them for hard labor. "I remember you and your raccoon eye from when you were a two-year-old. You were a real pain in the neck then; have you grown out of that?"

My face heats up. How do I respond? "I—I'm not perfect, but I think so."

Mother rushes to my aid. "She wasn't a pain in the neck; she was adorable. She is even more of a delight now."

Greggory rolls his eyes. "You see that, Brock? I was right. You are just as much of a pain in the neck now as you were then, maybe more so."

Brock approaches me and gives me a stiff hug, "Don't mind Greggory. He is afraid you will take all our parents' attention— and money. I'm sure they love us all equally though, right, Mom?"

Mother's usual composed manner is slipping away. "I don't know how we started the first conversation as a complete family in 14 years this way, but of course we love you all equally!"

Greggory laughs and shakes his head at me. He struts to the most comfortable chair in the room and sits down like he owns the place. I don't know what to say, so I just stand there awkwardly. Joy grabs my hand and pulls me over to the dolls she is playing with in the corner. I am happy for the distraction and follow her gladly.

I listen as Brock talks candidly to my parents. "You know that she is a fugitive, right? They will probably put a bounty on her head."

Greggory sits up straighter when he hears that. "How much do you think she's worth?"

Mother shows her power when she says, "It doesn't matter, Greggory, because if you turn her in, I will cut you off completely. You will never get another cent from me again."

Greggory snorts in disgust. "She was always your favorite—your only darling daughter."

"If you had been stolen from me, I would have said the same thing in your behalf. Family sticks together, Greggory."

"But should families break the law together?" Brock asks as he raises his eyebrows.

"Only if the law takes one of the family members away forever without consent!"

Brock puts a hand on Mother's arm. "Simmer down, Mom. I know that you have felt wronged since the day they took Elira to the complex, but you do realize that taking out the flaws in our society gives the future generations the best chance at long and healthy lives?"

Greggory mutters under his breath, "And gives you the cheap catering that you need for your political luncheons."

"Whose side are you on, Greggory?"

"My own, obviously."

Mother raises her eyebrows. "Brock, I find it very ironic that you think all of the flaws in our society have been eliminated. Do you consider pride, power-seeking, or the opposite, slothfulness and free-loading, human flaws? Because I do, and those flaws are running rampant everywhere I turn." I stifle a laugh. Wow, Mom isn't holding back.

I don't think Dad can take any more bickering. "Okay, everyone. Cook has made us a spectacular lunch. Let's go eat it while it's hot." Everyone grumbles but gets up and walks to the dining room. Everyone except me. I turn the opposite direction and start back toward the stairs when I feel a hand on my shoulder. "Elira, come eat with your family." My father's eyes are pained as he pleads with me.

"Dad, they don't feel like family. They obviously don't like me. I think everyone involved would feel much more comfortable if I ate downstairs."

"I wouldn't. I know they are spoiled, and rude, but they are your brothers. Please help us have one meal together as a complete family? For your Mom and Dad's sake?"

I cringe, but I let my father take my arm and lead me to the dining room. He seats me in between my mother and Joy. This is probably the safest seat for me, and I'm grateful. My father takes two plates from someone in the doorway and places a plate of—meat in front of me. I lean over to my mother. "What is this?"

"Filet mignon"

I don't know what that is, but it smells delicious. Joy taps my hand with her little fingers. "Help me?" The corners of my mouth turn up. How can I say no to that cute little face? I keep myself busy helping Joy cut her meat as her mother whispers conspiratorially with Brock.

Greggory glares at me across the table. Brock smiles at me, but the smile doesn't actually reach his eyes.

Father clears his throat. "Is there anything exciting going on that we can tell Elira about?"

Brock's wife, Chantilly, lights up for the first time since arriving. "La Blanca just opened its doors this week!" She gushes on and on about the new high-fashion clothing store that opened up in their city.

Brock opens his eyes super wide at Chantilly and then taps his watch. She nods at him and stops talking. Brock takes a deep breath. "Everyone, Chantilly and I actually have an announcement to make. Honey, would you like to do the honors?"

Chantilly nods and lets the corners of her mouth curl up a tiny bit. "We are pregnant."

My mother smiles and gushes, "Congratulations! How far along are you?"

"Three months."

I find my voice for long enough to say, "Congratulations; children are wonderful."

Brock and Chantilly both smile and nod at me. Greggory just glares at us all.

"I know a few excellent doctors in Adanlay that I would recommend."

Chantilly looks down her nose at my father. "We already have the best of the best doctors for me and for the baby once it's born. Thanks anyway." My father looks cowed.

Brock takes a big bite of his filet mignon and swallows it. "So, enough about us. Elira, how did you escape the complex of undesirables when no one else has in 40 years?"

I swallow what's in my mouth and think about how to respond. "Through the laundry and garbage chutes."

Greggory starts laughing uncontrollably.

Brock glares at his brother. "Shut up, Greggory. That must have been unpleasant, Elira. It looks like you broke your foot in the process."

"No, I was almost out when Mentor Briggs grabbed my foot. I kicked my shoe off, but he grabbed my toes. I kicked hard enough to break my toes and get away."

Greggory stops laughing. In fact, everyone falls silent.

"I hear you escaped with some friends. Did they convince you to do all of that unpleasantness?" Brock inquires.

I shake my head. "No, I was the one who figured out how to escape. I couldn't let them kill my best friend, Avra. My friends followed me."

Brock looks like he doesn't believe me. "Huh. Interesting."

Greggory pulls a flask out of his pocket and pours some kind of liquid into his lemonade. When my father sees what he is doing, he slaps the loosely-capped flask out of Greggory's hand. It flies across the table and clatters onto my empty plate. Greggory and Father start shouting at each other. Yikes. I'm not used to hearing raised male voices like this.

"Greggory, you're putting yourself in an early grave!"

"I am not! You're treating me like a baby." I quietly pick up the flask and screw the top on tightly. I hold the flask in my lap, hoping everyone will calm down if they don't look at it.

Brock pushes back from the table. "I think it's time for us to go. This was an interesting reunion. I'm sure we'll have another soon. Chantilly and Joy need a nice nap at the hotel."

"You don't have to stay at a hotel. Why don't you stay here?" Mother asks.

Chantilly opens her eyes as wide as they will go and shakes her head almost imperceptibly to her husband. He gets the hint. "No. Thank you. That is out of the question. You have a house full already."

"I don't need a nap, Papa!"

"Yes, you do, Sugar. We'll visit Grandma and Grandpa again soon."

Mother stands up. "Before you go, you must promise not to turn Elira or her friends in or tell anyone about anything we've talked about."

"Mother, this situation is really testing me as an enforcer of the law and a candidate for the Senate."

"Brock, she is family. You know the complex law is old-fashioned and unfair. The way they escaped is not for you to repeat to anyone or use in any political way."

Brock looks at me and softens slightly before he promises, "I won't tell a soul, Mom."

Greggory swears and throws a fit, but eventually promises not to tell when he is reminded that he will be completely cut off if he doesn't. "I can't believe my 'high moral' parents are asking me to break the law."

"I'd think you would like us more because of it," Dad mutters under his breath.

We all get up and move to the front door. I hide the flask in the pocket of my pants. With my mother's prompting, I give each of Brock's family members a hug. Joy's chubby little arms feel so nice around my neck. Brock and Chantilly hug me stiffly back and leave. The sunshine that falls on my face as the door opens and closes warms my troubled heart.

I give Greggory a hug despite his complaining and secretly slip the flask to him. He immediately stops grumbling and looks at me with a quizzical brow. I really don't understand what he has to complain about. He has such a good life. "Enjoy your time at the university, Greggory. I wish I could go there to learn, but obviously I can't. Maybe you could bring me a book to read when you're done with it. See you later." He doesn't say anything to me, and still looks perplexed as he waves half-heartedly and walks out the door.

Chapter 8

"ELIRA, DO YOU WANT TO GO OUTSIDE?" my mother asks as she leans over the back of the sofa.

I drop the history book I'm reading in my lap. "Yes! Of course, I do."

"I need to pick up a custom chess board I ordered. You guys can have a chess tournament if you have more than one board. The shop is located next to Complex Supply Row. I think that is something you should see."

"Is that where they sell the stuff my friends make in the complex?"

"Yes."

I sit up. "Yeah. I want to see it."

"I want to see it too. Can I come?" Jefrey asks from right beside me. I jump in surprise. Where did he come from? Was he eavesdropping on me?

Mother shrugs her shoulders. "One more won't cause a scene, but you're all I'm willing to take this trip. You two go get your disguises on."

Jefrey is positively giddy as he glues his fake black eyebrows and soul patch on.

"What are you so excited about, Jef?" Garth asks his brother suspiciously.

"I'm going to Complex Supplies Row with Elira."

"I want to come too."

"No. You can't. Florence said she's only taking the two of us."

"Why did she choose you?"

"She didn't, but I chose me. When you snooze, you lose, brother." Jefrey pats Garth on the shoulder. Garth throws his hand off and storms off to his room. I get a weak smile from him before he slams the door to his room.

Mother purses her lips as she watches the whole exchange. "All right, Elira, Jefrey, don't forget your sunglasses, and let's go."

She walks us to the garage and opens the driver side door

of a black car with four doors. Jefrey looks at the other cars in the garage before asking, "Can we take this white one instead?"

Mother shakes her head. "I think a sports car will draw too much attention to us right now. Let's stick with the easily-forgotten black sedan."

Jefrey frowns but then looks at me and smiles. I think he's pleased to have me to himself. He takes my hand and pulls me into the back of the car. I don't really want to hold his hand, so I let go quickly. I force a smile on my face and hope this trip will change his attitude toward the complex and everything else.

This is only the second vehicle I've ridden in. It is so much fancier than Ernestine's van. I hope my feet don't dirty the perfectly black floor. As we drive down the road, we see so many buildings of different shapes, sizes, and colors. I am in complete awe of the beauty that variety gives the outside world. We see a thin teenage boy about our age riding on a skinny, metal contraption with two wheels. It is so loud, I cover my ears. Jefrey can't take his eyes off the teenager. "What is that guy riding, Florence?"

"It's called a motorcycle. He should be wearing a helmet. Motor scooter crashes can be deadly."

"Are cars safer than motorcycles?"

"Yes. Cars have seatbelts, air bags, and metal to slow down an oncoming vehicle from hitting your body. Motorcycles don't have that."

Jefrey nods, always appreciating safety features. "If we ever get to live out of hiding, I'm going to get a sports car, except mine will be red."

Mother is silent for a minute as she thinks. "You never know, Jefrey, if you work hard and save your money, you could get an expensive car like that."

He looks confused. "Was your sport's car more expensive than this car?"

"Yes, much more expensive."

"Where do you buy a car?"

"At a dealership. It's a store for cars. Speaking of stores, we're here."

Mother parks next to a row of stores that touch sides and go on for half a mile on both sides of the street. The one we're closest to says 'Gail's Custom Woodworks' on the sign. The store next to it says 'Complex Cleaning Supplies.' My eye travels down the street and then moves to the other side of the street. The signs for Complex Paintings, Complex Catering, Complex Clothing Design, Complex Rugs and Carpets, Complex Cabinetry, Complex Steel, Complex Plastics, and Complex Linens stare back at me.

"I'm just going to pop in to Gail's Custom Woodworks and pick up my chess board. Why don't you two take a look in the windows of these stores while I'm gone?"

"Okay," Jefrey says cheerfully as we exit the car. He comes around to my side and takes my hand. I'm not feeling the zing I felt when he held my hand in the complex, but he's so happy, I just let him do it.

"I'll join you two in a few minutes."

"Okay, M—Mrs. Hamble."

Jefrey pulls me by the hand past Complex Cleaning Supplies and to the window of Complex Paintings. "Look at that red and black swirly one. I like it."

I focus in on each brush stroke of the red and black painting in the window. I wish I knew who painted it. I'm almost positive that they were unhappy when they created this piece. I see the darkness, despair, and the downward pull that the artist felt as they painted. It makes me feel like I might fall into the abyss with them. "Why do you like this one, Jefrey?"

"It looks the way I feel most days, swirling around in the dark."

"You don't have to feel that way. Look at this bright, yellow one. You could feel sunny and optimistic like this artist if you wanted."

His eyebrows crease. "I don't get to choose the way I feel."

"Yes, you do."

"No, I don't. How can I, when I have you and Garth irritating me all the time?"

I feel my blood start to boil. "You're choosing to be irritated."

"No, you're choosing to be irritating."

I roll my eyes in exasperation. "Whatever. Let's keep

moving." A sweet smell draws us to the next building. We practically press our noses against the Complex Catering window. The cinnamon rolls, cookies and cakes look delectable. A sign in the window lets us know that appetizers are buy one, get one half off this month.

"Those flower cookies look delicious. I'm going to ask how much they are." Jefrey bursts into the shop before I can stop him. I don't know what else to do, so—I follow him. He smiles at the shopkeeper. "Excuse me, ma'am, how much is one of these flower cookies?"

A tall, scrawny woman scratches her gray head with a pencil. "This isn't a bakery, sonny. This is a catering service. We don't sell anything individually. If you want a cookie, you'll have to buy them by the dozen."

"So, how much is a dozen?"

"Six dollars."

Jefrey nods as he takes in everything else in the display window. "Okay, I'll have to think about it." I'm relieved that the woman isn't calling the peace officers. She must not recognize us. I let out a long breath as I read the picture boards promoting sliced hams, turkeys and roasts. As we leave the store Jefrey asks me, "If it's six dollars for a dozen cookies, why won't she sell me one for 50 cents?"

I shrug. "Obviously she makes more money if you are required to buy more."

"I'm going to ask your mom for six dollars."

My feet stop walking. "Jefrey, what if Shasta made those cookies yesterday without pay?"

"I want to know if she's any good at it," he says nonchalantly.

"Hello, you two," My mom's voice says from behind us.

"Hi," I say unenthusiastically.

Mother looks in the window of Complex Catering and huffs. "How does seeing the work of your friends' unpaid hands make you feel?"

"Angry."

"Hungry. Can I have six dollars?" Jefrey asks. You have got to be kidding me.

Mother purses her lips and points to the car. "No. Absolutely not. If you want something to eat, we'll go home where our paid chef has lunch waiting."

Chapter 9

PEEKING THROUGH THE BLINDS, I see a fluffy white cat chasing a plastic bag blowing in the wind. I wonder how that fluff would feel on my fingertips. I point the cat out to Garth, who is sitting beside me. He puts his arm around me and scoots closer so we're cheek-to-cheek as we look through the little gap in the blinds. His cheek sends a jolt through mine as it bumps into me. I wonder what it would be like if he turned his head and...

"Elira, Garth, come join us at the computer desk," Mother yells across the basement, louder than is necessary. We reluctantly get up and join everyone at the computer desk in the corner of the great room. This enormous desk usually has one computer on it, but Mother has squished in two more. She squeezes my shoulder when I join her. "It's time to give you kids computer classes. Ernestine and I have many things on our minds and we'd like to pass the researching of your parents on to you. There are only three computers, so you'll have to take turns. Everyone, watch me and then you can try."

We learn that we can find information about my friends' parents using these funny light-up screens and keyboards. Avra takes these lessons much more seriously than I do. Unfortunately, her parents are the hardest to find anything about.

For three weeks we search these things called newspaper websites trying to find news articles about families struggling with the loss of their undesirable children. We look through thick books called phone-books hoping that a name will spark some kind of memory for Avra. It doesn't work. Ernestine sneaks out a few times, much to my mother's dismay, and talks to people who 'know things.' First names of undesirable children just aren't much to go on.

Avra, Jefrey, and I are sitting side by side at the computer desk when Jefrey sits straight up in his chair. His computer screen is open to a tabloid newspaper article about a mother who had twin boys taken away 14 years ago. Jefrey reaches over and squeezes my hand. I slip my hand out of his before he can say anything. "Elira, listen to this. 'Mrs. Yesterly said, 'taking two at once isn't fair.' While Mr. Yesterly insisted, 'If you take away my two kids, you should take away the hospital bill I still haven't paid as well. I shouldn't have to pay for kids I don't get to keep.' Huh. What do you think?"

I don't know how to respond, but I'm determined to be nice yet firm with Jefrey. "Well, the mother sounds sad that her twins were taken away. It could be them, but maybe not. You probably weren't the only twins in the complex." Garth and Rocky overhear us and leave their chess game to join us at the computers.

Rocky scans the article quickly. "There was only one other set of twins our age in the complex. They were reds and only lasted to age six or seven. I think it's a 50/50 chance that these are your parents."

Garth reads what the dad said over again. "I don't know if I should be happy that we may know who they are, or sad that my dad only cared about a money refund when he sent me away."

I spin around in my swively chair and punch Garth playfully in the arm. "I'll look up the present whereabouts of Mr. and Mrs. Yesterly. You and Jefrey should find the other set of parents of twin boys from 14 years ago."

Avra has been leaning on her arm, listening to us dispassionately. She stands up and yawns. "I've been looking for my parents for hours today, and I still haven't found a single thing." I detect a trace of jealousy in her voice. "I need a nap. Garth, you can use this computer." She walks sleepily back to our bedroom. I wish I could comfort her, but I promised the boys...

Garth sits down in Avra's empty seat. I have a twin on either side of me now. It's not as awkward as it used to be, but it still isn't a comfortable setting. Garth smiles at me and gets to work, Jefrey follows suit. Every time Garth's hand bumps into mine I feel tingles. When Jefrey's hand does the same thing, I don't feel—much of anything. I'm glad I have something to keep me busy.

I'm surprised at how easy it is to find Mr. Bart and Mrs. Wiona Yesterly. They appear to be at the same address that they lived at when their twins were taken away. An hour goes by and Garth bumps me with his shoulder. "Look at this. This medical journal from 16 years ago says that Herrington Hospital has seen an increase in twins of deformity this year. The hospital has delivered one set of deformed female twins and two sets of deformed male twins this year which is triple what they would normally expect."

I shake my head. "It's probably just luck. There are no toxins deforming people out here."

Garth nods. "They intended to study the three families in depth to find out what they have in common."

"Do they give any names?"

"No, but they do refer to family A, S, and Y."

Jefrey jumps into our conversation. "A, S, and Y, you say? I read an article yesterday about deformed twin Swenson girls from 14 years ago being taken to the complex. Swenson, S, and Yesterly, Y. The other twin boys must be from a family that starts with A."

Ernestine overhears us from the couch and joins in. "If you know their name starts with an A, just look up the government complex records from that year. They don't give out much information, but if you know where to look there is a list of affected last names in alphabetical order."

I immediately pull the complex website up. Ernestine directs me through several menus to find the affected families list. At the top of the list I find three last names that start with A. "So the other twin boy parents must be the Adams, the Aichers, or the Addlesons."

"It's not the Addlesons. I remember them vaguely from that day. They were uncooperative like me. They had a girl though," Ernestine says, her deep alto voice going deeper with repressed feelings.

"So it's the Adams or the Aichers."

"Give me your computer, Garth." Ernestine kicks Garth out of his chair. "I'll just look both of them up, and the Yesterlys too." Ernestine is a computer whiz when she knows the last names of whom she's looking for. She writes down the Adams', Aichers', and Yesterlys' addresses on a piece of paper, grabs a blonde, curly wig and a backpack, and leaves without a word.

Jefrey swivels around to face Garth, Rocky, and me. "Should we have tried to stop her?"

Rocky shakes his head. "I don't think it would do any good. She's sick of being cooped up in here. She likes to be outside snooping around."

I raise my eyebrows. "I doubt my Mom will like it." Jefrey nods in agreement.

Rocky shrugs. "I know. I don't think any of us could stop her though, so, oh well. Let's finish our chess game, Garth."

They move back to the coffee table, Garth squeezing my shoulder as he passes me. Jefrey turns to me. I can tell he wants to say something, but he isn't sure that I'll like it. He can't help himself. "Ernestine takes too many unnecessary risks. We should have stopped her. She should talk to Florence before taking off like that."

I lean back in my chair and yawn. "Oh well. Ernestine does what she feels is right, and what she feels is right has done nothing but help me. You should trust her."

"Trusting people is a risky business, Elira."

"That's true." This is the longest conversation I've had with Jefrey in quite a while. I usually lose my patience and leave.

"What did you think of your brothers a few weeks ago? I haven't had the chance to ask you."

"Yeah. They are—interesting."

"They are probably talking to their friends about your escape right now."

96

I shake my head. "I doubt it. My mom made them promise not to. *Yawn*. I'm taking a quick nap before dinner. See you later."

"But we could count money together..."

"Nope. See you at dinner." I smile at Garth as I walk back to my room. Scott takes my seat at the computer as I leave.

AVRA SHAKES ME VIOLENTLY to wake me up. "Elira! Scott thinks he's found his parents!"

"That's great. I'll celebrate with you guys after my nap."

"Of course you're not excited. You have your parents back already." Avra turns away from me and huffs. "I'll tell you about it later."

I feel like a jerk. "No, Avra. Come back. I'm sorry. It is exciting news. We've been working so hard for this. Tell me about it." I sit up and wipe the sleep from my eyes with a smile.

"Scott found an article with first and last names. Come see!"

I groan internally and push myself out of bed. I make the bed quickly so it's not obvious that someone is staying in here. I force a smile for Avra and follow her to the great room.

Scott is usually so quiet, but he whoops with delight as we approach him. He beckons us to hurry over to the computer. "This article says that Lola and Mick Taylor, the parents of

'Undesirable Scott Taylor' were told they would be fined $5000 dollars if they sent another letter of protest to the government complex committee." Scott looks at us all expectantly. "Don't you see? They protested. They might want me back!"

I smile and pat Scott on the back. "That's great, Scott!"

Mother leans over Scott's back to read the article for herself. "Lola and Mick Taylor. If or when Ernestine gets back, we'll have her investigate them. Did you find an address for them, Scott?"

"Yes. Of course I did. It's right here." Scott waves a lined piece of paper in the air with triumph.

Mom takes the paper and looks at it. "Huh. That's not far from here. I think this may be one of the houses Ernestine watched the other day. She could walk there in ten minutes. Well, if she gets back here safely, anyway." Mother isn't happy Ernestine left without consulting her again.

My stomach growls. "I'm hungry. Is it dinnertime yet, Mom?"

Mother looks at the clock. "Oh, yes. Your chicken cordon bleus have been getting cold for 20 minutes. Will you help me bring the food down, Elira?"

"Yes."

Garth follows us to the stairs. "I'll help too." He smiles as he bumps my shoulder with his.

We walk behind my mother side by side up the stairs to the kitchen. I've never been in the main kitchen before. I stop in my tracks as I enter the big, beautiful room. Mother's short, plump cook has her back to us as she chops some greens on a cutting board.

I grab my mom's arm and whisper, "Mother, she shouldn't see us."

"She knows that my 'helpers' have secrets, Elira."

The cook turns around just then and I gasp as I see that half of the woman's face is covered in lumpy scars. "How can this be?" I ask.

Mother clears her throat. "Elira, I would like you to meet our cook, Freda. She used to work at the number one rated restaurant in the city, but after a grease fire burned her severely, she lost her job. Freda has worked for me ever since."

I look at Freda cautiously. "Do you know who I am?"

Freda looks at me and Garth and nods. "Yes. Everyone knows who you are."

"You've seen us on the news?"

"Yes."

"Will you turn us in?"

"No. I don't persecute people based on their appearance."

I take a few steps toward Freda and offer her my hand the way Ernestine taught us. "It's nice to meet you. Did they fire you because you couldn't work while you healed, or because you are scarred?"

Freda sets her knife down and wipes her lettuce juice-covered hand on her apron so she can take my hand. "I was told

I could have my job back after I was released from the hospital, but as soon as my boss saw my face, he said his business could not risk losing its high-class reputation because of my appearance."

"That is ridiculous."

"I agree. I was rarely seen by customers in the kitchen. It's okay though. I love working here. The pace is slower, and your parents are the best people I have ever known."

Mother pats Freda on the back. "I read Freda's story in a newspaper and immediately wrote to her to offer her a job here."

I look at my mother and feel my heart swell with pride. "My best friend, Avra, loves to cook. Will you teach her a few things?"

Freda's face breaks into a smile. "I would love to. I haven't had a student who can tolerate my presence since my accident. It would be nice to cook with someone again."

Garth steps forward. "We have eaten so well since we arrived here. Thank you for feeding us. What can I do to help?"

Freda has Garth and me sprinkle herbs on the chicken and croutons on the salad. Every time our hands bump into each other, a surge of heat goes up my arm. I feel Garth's eyes on me more than once. Freda smiles as she watches us. We laugh and tease each other as we take the food down to the basement.

Dinner tastes amazing to my empty stomach. I have a new appreciation for how such wonderful food finds its way to my plate. I just wish Ernestine was here to enjoy it with us. My mother is getting worried again. I can tell.

"Rocky, dear, would you mind flipping the lights on behind you? I can barely see my plate anymore," my mother says with a scowl. Rocky flips the light on.

Knock, knock. We all run to the bookshelf with the hidden door behind it. When the door is shut, I hear the outside door burst open. "Ernestine Moore, you can't keep running off without a word like that."

"I told the kids where I was going. Didn't they tell you?"

"Yes. They said you were going to look for the twins' potential parents, but I need to be in on your plans. If something goes wrong, I'll be the one left to pick up the pieces."

"I would have been back before dark, but there are still a lot of peace officers patrolling the streets. I had to move slowly."

"Let's let the kids out."

Click. Ernestine's face is a welcome sight, but it doesn't give us any hints. Garth speaks first, "How many houses did you watch tonight?"

"Two. The Yesterlys and the Adams. I'll tell you all about it while I eat my dinner."

Ernestine tells us between bites of chicken cordon bleu and green salad that the Adams are definitely not the twins' parents. "They don't look anything like you two. Different races even." She only saw a dark-haired Mrs. Yesterly at the Yesterly house.

"There is some potential for shared genes there, but I'm not sure at this point."

Scott can't hold his news back any longer. "I found my parents, Ernestine! Lola and Mick Taylor. They were almost fined for sending protest letters. They might want me back!"

"Excellent! I will check them out tomorrow morning on the way to the Aichers."

"Thank you for telling me now, not after, Ernestine," Mother says dryly.

Ernestine smiles at my mother in her toothy way. "No problem."

My friends are hard to wind down before bed. It's been an exciting day. I just hope the good news continues in the morning.

Chapter 10

"CHECKMATE." I don't think Garth can concentrate on our chess game very well with Ernestine outside investigating his potential parents. She's been gone for the last five hours.

"Oh, you win. Good job, Elira."

"Garth, are you okay?"

"Yeah. Well—I can't stop thinking about my parents. Do you think they'll like me?"

What a silly question. "Yes, I do. You are the easiest person in the world to like."

"I don't agree with that," Jefrey grumbles under his breath.

Knock, knock. Mother stops us from running. "Just wait. I'll peek through the blinds, and if it's Ernestine, you don't have to hide." Mother uses two fingers to peek through the blinds. Garth looks like he's going to fall on his face, he's leaning forward so far. "It's her. You're safe."

We all breathe a sigh of relief as Ernestine comes through the door. "Did you save any lunch for me, Florence?"

"Yes. There is a sandwich in the fridge."

Ernestine sits down at the table with her sandwich and starts chowing down on it.

Garth and Jefrey wrestle each other to sit next to her. "So?" Garth asks.

Ernestine swallows down a bite. "The Taylors are definitely Scott's parents." Scott jumps up and pumps his fist with excitement. "I'm about 95% sure that the Yesterlys are your parents." Garth breathes a sigh of relief and relaxes both of his clenched fists.

"When are we going to talk to them?" Jefrey asks hesitantly.

"I don't have a great feeling about them yet, Jefrey. There's a weird aura hovering over that house. We'll approach Scott's parents first, I think."

Garth and Jefrey look at each other uncertainly. "Okay," Garth says.

"I am not thrilled about how much surveillance each

house is getting still. Let's give it another week and then we'll approach Scott's parents."

ERNESTINE IS DISGUISED AS A MAN today. It makes me laugh every time I look at her. She thinks the neighbors might be getting suspicious of her visits to the Taylors' neighborhood, so she changed her look. Rocky is sick. He has been in bed or in the bathroom all morning long. He won't be going with us. Ernestine says I can only go with the 'approach group' if I can walk without my bulky boot. I take that thing off so fast, Garth smiles at my eagerness. I have had very little time outside, and more painfully, very little time alone with Garth. Between my mother and Jefrey, we always seem to have a chaperone. I really want him to hold my hand again. I'm sure we can on the walk to Scott's parents' house. Avra probably wants to hold Scott's hand on the walk today, too. Unfortunately, she is having a bad health day. Her heart is beating irregularly, and she keeps having to sit down. Ernestine says she can't come.

I fill with compassion as I watch Avra hug Scott goodbye. "Avra, maybe you could sit on a chair in the kitchen and have a cooking lesson with Freda after your nap today," I say encouragingly. She nods sadly, squeezes Scott's hand, then goes to our room and cries. I wish I could do something more for her, but she doesn't have the strength today—and I really want to go outside.

I coat my raccoon eye with flesh colored makeup and put my sunglasses on. I try to walk without a limp as we leave the house. Mother reaches out and takes my arm. "Are you sure your toes can keep up, Elira?"

I know that my toes will still slow me down, but I want to go outside so much. "My toes feel great, Mother. Please let me go."

She sees the longing in my eyes and sets her concerns aside. "Don't let Ernestine do anything risky. Remember the telephone number we had you memorize. Call me if you get separated, or if anything goes wrong."

"Okay. I will."

"Be careful, Elira," Mother calls as I shut the door behind me. The rush of the wind in my hair invigorates me. The air out here is positively delicious to inhale. How have I breathed stale indoor air my whole life? I feel Garth's hand brush up against mine. Yay, he waited for me! He switches sides with me so his normal hand is next to mine. I look over at him in his fake ear and sideburns, and a smile erupts on my face as he slides his fingers in between mine. I don't care about my aching toes; I could walk all day now. As we walk down the sidewalk, the headline of a discarded newspaper grabs my eyes. "$100,000 Reward for the Capture of the Complex Escapees." I see Jefrey looking at the paper a little longer than he should as we walk by. We've never seen a bill that is more than $50. It's hard to imagine what $100,000 in bills would look like.

Ernestine barks out, "Jefrey, pick that paper up and throw it away. Florence hates litter around her house, and I hate the message that paper portrays. People are more likely to turn you in now that there is a reward." Scott is already nervous about meeting his parents, but now I can see his hands visibly shaking. Ernestine pats Scott on the back. "Don't be nervous, though. I need you to look like walking down the street is the most natural thing ever to you." Jefrey picks up the paper but he folds it up and sticks it in his jacket pocket.

Ernestine takes one last look behind us as we walk on. "There's no peace officer watching the house," she says with astonishment.

I love looking at the colorful buildings, but I think Garth likes looking at the different kinds of cars parked on the street more. He points out a fancy blue car with no top on it as we walk. The man who owns it is washing or maybe just polishing it. He looks up and waves at us as he sees Garth admiring it. "I like your car," Garth calls out.

"If you like it, you'll be interested to know I'm putting it up for sale after I'm done detailing it."

Jefrey stops walking and calls out, "How much is it?"
"$25,000."

Garth whistles. "That's more than I have, but it's beautiful. Good luck selling it."

"Thanks, kid. Have a good day."

Ernestine claps Garth and Jefrey on the shoulders as we walk on. "Good job, boys. That was a very normal conversation. I don't think he knew you were complex escapees at all."

The twins smile at each other, which is nice to see. Ernestine observes the house of Scott's parents as we approach it a few minutes later. "There are no peace officers watching the house here either. How strange," Ernestine mutters under her breath. Butterflies fill my stomach as we pause at their white, wooden front gate. Ernestine lets out a long breath. "Scott, are you ready for this?" He is twisting his hands together nervously as he nods. "We cannot tell them where we are staying. If they seem like they might turn us in, we will have to run for it. Promise me you'll do exactly what I say if something goes wrong."

"Okay, I promise," Scott says and the rest of us echo him.

His fumbling hands open the gate and he walks through it. We follow closely behind him. He leads us to the front door of a blue, squarish house with white shutters. He pauses for a moment, then knocks on the door. A man who looks like an older version of Scott opens the door. He looks at Scott through the screen door for a minute. Then he looks at the rest of us. Scott pulls off his false nose and says, "Hello, Father. It's me, Scott."

The man's chocolatey brown face scrunches up and he starts crying. "I can't believe it. Come in, come in!" We all pile into the midsized house. Scott's mother walks in just then; she is holding a girl who looks about Joy's age. She sets the girl down and runs to Scott, throwing her arms around him.

"I knew it! I knew you'd find us!"

Scott's usually-controlled face breaks into tears. His father wraps his arms around the two of them and cries with his wife and long-lost son. I feel my heart overflowing as I watch the reunited family. The government is cruel to take us away from people who love us like this. We should be hugged and kissed and cried over. Garth, Jefrey, Ernestine and I creep quietly around them and seat ourselves on the gently-worn sofa and armchairs nearby. When the tear-stained family breaks out of the hug, Scott's father says, "They have been watching the house for weeks. We were afraid they might have captured you. But then the news today says that they are offering a reward for your capture. It made it seem like they hadn't found you."

Ernestine looks at Mick Taylor. "They don't know where we are, and we intend to keep it that way."

Scott slides a finger around the top of his turtleneck shirt. "I've been staying somewhere safe and comfortable. We've been waiting for the watching peace officers to leave."

His mother gently pulls the turtleneck down a little so she can see Scott's lumpy neck. "Your neck isn't that bad. I was so upset when they took you away. I wrote letters of protest. Unfortunately, there was nothing we could do."

Scott's tear-stained lips smile. "I know. I'm just happy to meet you."

Lola Taylor starts bawling hysterically. "I wish you remembered me."

He hugs his mom again. "Don't cry. This feels familiar, but I don't remember life before the complex."

Lola looks Scott over as if expecting to find bruises. "Did they hurt you?"

Scott looks at me before answering his mother. "Not physically, but it was mentally hard at times. I tried not to cause trouble. If I had stayed in the complex one more year, I would have had a job nine hours a day, seven days a week of hard labor. My life was about to become—grim."

"I'm so glad you got out when you did. You won't be able to stay long; the officers are coming here for a meeting in an hour. But you have to meet your sisters."

Ernestine leans forward in her chair. "We can't risk having little mouths saying things to their friends that will get us captured."

Lola frowns then perks up. "We can call him a cousin then. Will that work?"

Ernestine pauses before she nods. "Just keep your story consistent in front of them."

Lola nudges the little girl hanging on her arm forward. "This little one is Ann, and I'm pretty sure Laura is in the kitchen. She is ten and doesn't like company. She's very shy."

Scott's father brings out the shy ten-year-old and Scott hugs the two girls. "Hi, girls. I'm your cousin... Seth. I'm so happy to meet you."

The girls smile shyly at him. Ann looks him in the eyes. "Mom said you can't stay long. Will you visit us again?"

"Yes. I will visit you as often as I can."

"Okay, good." Ann smiles at Scott in the most heart-melting way.

Mr. Taylor takes the girls into the kitchen for some milk and cookies. Mrs. Taylor hugs Scott again and then cradles his face in her hands. I can barely hear her whisper, "Scott, I want you to know that we were heartbroken when they took you away from us. There was nothing we could do. When all the excitement dies down, we would like you to move back in with us. We have so much to catch up on."

Through his tears, Scott says, "I will. I will move back in as soon as it is safe. I will have to live in hiding, but I want to know you. I want to know my family."

Mr. Taylor rubs Scott's head of cornrows affectionately with his hand. "You will, Scott. I wish you could stay longer, but I don't want to risk the peace officers seeing you. If you can, come by on Fridays at noon. I only work half a day on Fridays, and the officers have a big weekly lunch and powwow on the other side of town. It'll be the safest time for now."

"Okay. I will be here Friday at noon."

Scott's parents hug him again, and his mother kisses his

cheeks about twenty times. We all feel warm and fuzzy as we leave. Scott has a hard time keeping his emotions in check as we walk home. He keeps saying, "They love me," and, "They want me back."

I punch him playfully in the arm. "Of course they want you back. I know someone else who probably wants you back right now too."

Suddenly a peace officer with a thick gray mustache walks out of a house in front of us. He looks at us curiously as he approaches his car. Ernestine nods at him and says, "Nice day, officer." We make a sharp right turn and then another quick left turn down the alley. Ernestine whispers to us as she signs with her hands. *Hide, now. And be quiet.* We probably aren't thinking clearly, but we quickly find places to hide. Ernestine climbs up the side of a broken-down building like a spider and slips in a broken window. The twins and Scott hide in an abandoned van that has been left to rot in the alleyway. I won't fit in there with them. Jefrey points to big, black bags of garbage beside the van. Oh, gag. I don't have time to find anything else so I shift the stinky, lumpy bags on top of myself.

The officer turns down the alley in his car. I understand why Ernestine was so quiet now. I'm pretty sure his window is down because I hear him snort and spit on my garbage bags. Gross! I try not to wiggle or gag. The tires of his vehicle pause just past the garbage heap I'm hiding in. Luckily, he doesn't exit his vehicle. I try not to breathe as I hear the tires roll past me.

My heart is beating so fast, I worry that the whole city can hear it.

Crack, tinkle, tinkle. It sounds like a window has broken around the corner from where we came. The officer backs his car down the alley and turns toward the sound of broken glass and zips off.

"Let's go now, kids!" Ernestine yells out as she scampers down the side of the building. We run straight down the alleyway and then try to walk quickly without drawing attention to ourselves once we get to the main street. I am going as fast as I can, but my tender toes make me slower than everyone else. Ernestine turns around and looks at me with concern.

"You can leave me behind, Ernestine. Just get them to safety."

She laughs at me. "And face your mother without you? No way. You can do it, we're almost there." She takes my arm and pulls me forward.

I am gasping for air by the time we collapse inside the basement door of my parents' house. "Elira, are you okay?" my mother asks with alarm.

If she knew that a peace officer was tailing us, she probably won't let me out again. "Yes, I'm fine. I'm just out of shape. I really should exercise more."

My mother doesn't believe me. "Ernestine, what happened? Why are you all exhausted?"

"Oh, no big deal, we just thought we saw a peace officer, so we decided to move a little faster."

My mother stares hard at Ernestine, who refuses to meet her gaze. "Look! My favorite soup. Let's eat!"

We all take Ernestine's hint and sit down at the table, trying not to look confused or shocked. Avra sits next to Scott and asks, "So, how was it, Scott? Were your parents nice?"

Scott positively lights up and hugs Avra. "Yes, they were kind and loving, and they want me back! My mother kissed my cheeks over and over again. I think I kind of remember her doing that. It felt so—right."

Avra smiles at him and sighs, "I can't wait until I get to meet my parents. It'll be just like that I bet."

Chapter 11

SCOTT ONLY GETS TO BE THE CENTER of attention for two days. Ernestine goes by herself to observe the Yesterlys again. When she gets back, Garth insists that we are ready to meet the twins' parents.

"I'm not 100% sure they are the right people, Garth."

"You said you were 95% sure though."

"Yeah, I think it's them, but they aren't like Scott's parents."

Garth is insistent. "Every parent is going to be different, Ernestine. I want to meet them."

Ernestine is a little bit reluctant after the close call we had the other day, but she finally gives in. Garth is excited. Jefrey is nervous, of course. Everything makes him nervous. Mother doesn't really want me to go, but she doesn't stop me. Rocky and Avra aren't feeling well again, so they will be staying here. Scott says he'll stay with Avra to keep her company. That means it'll just be Ernestine, Garth, Jefrey, and me. Yikes. I hope I can tolerate the love triangle I've placed myself in.

Ernestine is disguised as a woman with her fake chin today. She's decided that we need to approach this visit differently. "If we see a peace officer or anyone suspicious this time, we are not going to run. We have to learn to talk our way out of trouble."

"What do we say?" Jefrey asks.

"I've made up a fake name and story for each of you. Elira, you are Edith Westergard, niece to Doctor Hamble. You are an 18-year-old student of pharmaceuticals. You are visiting your uncle for the weekend."

"Okay, I'll do my best."

"Garth, you are Garrett Shofield. You're 19 years old and a student of medicine. You are being mentored by Doctor Hamble."

"Sure. Am I from here?"

"Uh, you don't know how to get around town, so we better say no. You are from Wellington. You are just visiting to shadow Doctor Hamble."

"Okay."

"Jefrey, you are Jack Dodge, 18 years old and an apprentice to an electrician. You are helping your boss fix an electrical problem at the Hamble's residence. Well, only say that if you are seen here. If you are seen anywhere else, say you're fixing an electrical problem at the museum."

"Why does Garth get to be older than me?"

"We need to make you two as unlike twins as possible."

"I want to be older."

Ernestine rolls her eyes. "Garth, is it okay if you are 18 and Jefrey is 19?"

Garth's lip curls as he looks at his brother's smug face. "Whatever."

"Great. Think of as many details as you can for the character you are playing. If a stranger asks your opinion on something, be ready with a response."

We practice having a conversation as our fake characters with my mom. "What do you mean you don't know if you like ice cream or not, Jack?"

"I've never had any."

"You have to pretend like you have and own your answer. Either say 'yes, I like ice cream' or 'no, I don't care for it,' It doesn't matter what you choose, just be confident in your answer when you aren't sure what they're talking about."

"Okay. I don't care for ice cream. I prefer cookies."

"That's better." Mother still doesn't look incredibly convinced when it's time to go.

I make sure I'm the last one out the door. Ernestine leads the way, with Jefrey by her side, pestering her with questions. I hang back a few steps, and Garth pauses his stride to match mine. I reach out and take his hand. He looks at me with excited, disguised-brown eyes. The sun is warm, the air is fresh, and I wish this walk would never end. Unfortunately, it does end, and rather quickly. Ernestine takes us to the big shop at the back of the property and opens the garage door. The shiny black car with four doors is in there instead of the garage. "Get in. The twins' parents live too far away to walk."

"How long will the drive be?" Garth asks.

"About 25 minutes; they live in the country."

Ernestine climbs into the driver seat. I motion at Garth to get in the back with me. I slide in the side door and he slides in right behind me. Unfortunately, Jefrey does not climb in the front passenger seat like I hoped he would. He climbs in the back on my other side. My hand that is holding Garth's lets go. I fold my arms in front of me instead. Jefrey smiles at me and starts rambling on about how nervous he is.

I try to catch Garth's eye, but he is looking out the window in his own little world. I'm sure both twins are wound as tight as springs inside. I hope this visit goes as well as Scott's did.

As we drive into the country, we pass fields of green plants and fields of big animals. I'm pretty sure the animals are cows. A grouping of houses surrounded by trees appears ahead of us. We pull up to a small, yet reasonably-fancy white house with an enormous green yard. A young boy, I'm guessing about age nine, is swinging on a swing connected to a tree branch. The tree is huge and old, yet healthy and charming. When the boy sees us pull into the driveway, he runs inside the house.

Ernestine turns around. "Did you see that kid? He looks just like you two! This has to be your parents' house!"

Garth smiles and jumps out of the car. Jefrey looks green. He slowly opens his door and just as slowly gets out. I sit there in the middle of the back seat for a moment. The car door on either side of me is open. I have to exit out one of them. I get out of Garth's door and shut it. I walk around the car to the other side and shut that door too because Jefrey didn't do it.

Garth speed walks to the front door of the white house before I can hold his hand. The rest of us follow behind him, much slower. Garth knocks on the door. It opens quickly to reveal the boy we saw on the swing.

"Hi, I'm Garrett. Who are you?"

The boy looks Garth over carefully before answering, "I'm Joseph. You look kind of familiar. Do you live around here?"

Garth smiles at the miniature version of himself. "Are your parents home, Joseph?"

"Not yet, they had to take some tree trimmers back to the neighbor. They should be back any minute."

"Is it okay if we wait for them?"

"I guess so. Do you want to play catch with me?"

Garth looks at his little brother affectionately. "Yes, we can play catch while we wait for them."

"I'll go get Mom and Dad's mitts. You guys go wait by the swing."

"Okay."

Jefrey leans over to Garth. "Do you know what mitts are?"

"No idea. But if it's called 'catch' I'm sure it's easy enough to figure out."

We all sigh with relief as we walk to the swing. Joseph is super cute and friendly. I sit down and start swinging back and forth. Garth smiles at my beaming face. He gives me a big push. It startles me yet exhilarates me too. I become very aware of the gravity and air current around me; it's amazing. I let him push me a few times, then insist that he try it. I jump off the swing. Garth goes to sit down, but pauses as he looks down at the wooden seat. Etched in the wood, it says, "Happy Birthday, Garth and Jefrey. Love, Grandpa."

"Jefrey, take a look at this."

"This has to be the right place."

Garth runs his fingers over the words. "I wonder if this Grandpa is still alive."

Joseph joins us with the mitt things he was talking about. "Wait, did you just call him, Jefrey?"

Garth gives Ernestine an apologetic look as he nods. "Yes, I did. Is your grandpa still alive?"

"Yes, but we can't visit him anymore. He lives in the Complex for the Elderly."

I watch Garth's face harden with anger and disappointment. "Was he sick when he went there?"

"No, not really. He played catch with me the day before he left."

Garth's eyes fill with emotion. Joseph looks at him curiously. "Why do you care about my grandpa?"

"I—I'm related to him too." Ernestine gives Garth a warning look.

Joseph looks at the inscription on the swing seat and then looks at the twins. The wheels are definitely turning in his head. Garth looks at Joseph and asks, "Do you know who we are, Joseph?"

"Garrett and Jefrey," Joseph mutters and then looks at the swing seat again. "Are you—my brothers?"

Jefrey smiles for the first time in a long time as he answers him, "Yes, we are." Ernestine shakes her head.

"But Mom and Dad said you died when you were two and a half." I hear footsteps approaching us on the gravel driveway.

"Hello, there. May I help you folks?" A man with dirty-blonde hair and broad shoulders asks from the driveway. His dark-haired, chubby wife stands cautiously behind him.

Jefrey approaches his father and mother at a faster pace than I think he should. "I'm Jefrey, your son. Why did you tell my little brother that we were dead?"

His father stumbles back several steps. "Wiona, call the authorities, now."

"NO!" Everyone else in the yard screams at once.

The nine-year old jumps up and down as he faces his father. "Dad, these are my brothers. They aren't dead. Let's invite them in!"

"They are wanted persons."

The woman takes her husband's hand. "Bart, look closely at them. I can see our features; they are our sons. It's like they have come back from the dead! I've missed them so. I want to talk to them."

The twins' dad does not budge. "We promised the authorities that we would not do that."

Wiona Yesterly stomps her foot. "I don't care what the authorities want. They have never cared about what I want." She pulls on her husband's arm in frustration. "Bart, these boys are your own flesh and blood. Come on, everybody. Let's go inside and have some lemonade."

"If we feed them, or take them in, we could be charged with aiding and abetting..."

"Shut up, Bart. Let's go inside, everyone."

Ernestine and I look at each other warily. Can we trust these people? Will the mom or the dad win out? We hesitantly decide to follow the divided family inside the house. We are led into a lovely sitting room with comfortable leather furniture. Joseph sits beside Garth and can't stop looking at him. Jefrey and their dad, Bart, keep glaring at each other across the room. Ernestine and I look at the mom for some assurance.

Wiona is the one who breaks the uncomfortable silence. "Your hair color is so different than I would have expected. You two used to be identical."

Garth leans toward her. "It's been dyed. These sideburns, earlobes, and eyebrows are all fake. We have to live in disguise now." He pulls off his fake sideburns and eyebrows.

His mom watches him and nods. "That makes sense." She takes Garth's deformed hand and gently examines it. "Garth," she looks across the room to her other son, "Jefrey, I am your mother. My name is Wiona Yesterly, this is your father, Bart Yesterly, and this is your little brother, Joseph." The family nods at each other, except for Bart. He just grunts. No hugging here. Mrs. Yesterly continues, "I have had a hole in my heart every day since they took you away. Bart thought it would be better for us all if we pretended that you boys had died. So that's what we told Joseph when he was old enough to understand."

"What? Who took them away? Where have they been?" Joseph asks.

Bart speaks up, "The government took them away to live in a complex full of other messed up kids." Jefrey jumps to his feet at that comment. Ernestine and I grab his arms and set him back down.

Joseph punches the arm of the couch with his fist. "I hate complexes. One took my grandpa away, so I can't visit him, and one took my brothers away, so I have no one to play with." Ernestine winks at Joseph.

Garth's voice is pained as he asks, "Father, do you honestly think our 'flaws' are bad enough that we should be shut away from the world in a work house?"

Before he can answer, Wiona jumps in, "Absolutely not. We were heartbroken when they deemed you unfit. They are wrong to take kids like you two away, with only minor flaws."

Garth isn't satisfied with that answer. "But are they right to take away the kids with major flaws?"

Wiona is speechless. Bart barges his way into the conversation. "Of course, they are! Flawed people aren't smart enough to realize that they shouldn't reproduce." Jefrey jumps to his feet again. Ernestine and I ease him back down a second time.

Their mother looks at her hands sheepishly. "It's so hard to know what is best for society anymore. I don't think the Complex Law is fair or right though."

Bart punches the arm of his chair. "The Complex Law makes life better for those healthy enough to keep our society thriving. If a person will be a burden or a disgrace to our society, they should go to the complex."

Jefrey jumps to his feet yet again. "You are calling me a disgrace. I could beat you at anything, old man." Bart bristles as he squeezes the arms of his armchair.

Wiona tries to calm the room down. "Bart has some

very strong opinions because of the propaganda that the government rams down our throats, but deep inside he is your father, and he does love you as much as I do."

"Speak for yourself, Wiona!"

Garth's mother slaps her knee. "Bart, why don't you and I go get the lemonade for everyone?"

"I would rather..."

She stands up with a deep frown on her face and hauls Bart out of his seat by the hand. "We will be right back with the lemonade. Joseph, would you keep our guests company while we are gone?"

"Sure, Mom." Joseph smiles at me and winks. He really is the cutest little boy. He looks like a younger version of Garth and Jefrey before they changed their appearance, with a little bit of mischief and secret delight thrown in.

"Don't listen to Dad. He likes to throw fits quite often, but Mom always talks him down. He'll see reason soon. You'll see."

Garth rubs his hands together nervously. "I hope so, or we won't be able to visit again. There is a reward for turning us in, and we are never going back to the complex."

"Was it horrible there?"

"No," Jefrey says.

Garth wraps his arm around Joseph. "It wasn't horrible per se. They were considerate more than kind to us, but our whole lives were a big lie. They told us that the world was toxic and that's why we had deformities. They said we were lucky that our parents had paid a whole bunch of money to get us into the complex where we could be safe."

"Holy moly. That is sad, but awesome!"

"Joseph, you can't tell anyone about us. Not your friends, not your teachers, no one. If anyone figures out who we are, they'll send us back to the complex."

"I won't tell anyone. I want you to come back as much as you can."

"If anyone asks about us, you tell them that we're friends, Garrett and Jack, from Wellington."

"Okay, I will. I know how to keep secrets. I will be your spy."

Ernestine laughs to herself. She'll have to explain what a spy is to us later.

The twins' parents walk in with trays of lemonade just then. Bart is much more subdued and helpful as he silently offers us a drink. Wiona seems relieved.

She pats the sofa next to Garth. "Jefrey, come sit by your brother. I want to show you two something." Jefrey obediently sits by the brother he isn't fond of. She hands Garth and Jefrey a thick book. "Here are all the photos I have of you two before you were taken. Look at how happy we all were."

I watch the twins as they look at pictures of their past. Joseph leans in and makes lots of his own comments about their surroundings. Their mother looks over their shoulders and adds comments now and then. I can see love and happiness in her eyes as she observes the three of them together. Bart seems to be struggling inside. The expressions on his face keep going from anger to acceptance to fear to sadness. Life is complex sometimes; there is no doubt about it.

Wiona touches the purple splotch between Jefrey's fingers. He flinches away. "You are handsome, Jefrey, despite your flaws."

"I know, thanks."

Garth looks at his brother and shakes his head. Wiona looks at Garth's stuck-together fingers again. "That hand will be noticed. How will you hide it?"

"I have pockets in all of my pants. I'll be just fine. It's my earlobe that might be a problem."

"What's wrong with your earlobe?" Garth pulls the fake one off and shows her. His mother gasps. "How did that happen?"

"A complex guard shot it off when we escaped."

Wiona hides her mouth with her hand. "Are you okay?"

"Yeah, D—someone stitched it up for me. It's practically healed now."

"That is the most terrible thing I've ever heard. Maybe you shouldn't have escaped."

Garth looks at his mom with pity. "If I had the chance to go back and change things, I would do it all again." His eyes turn to me. My heart beats faster as I remember the blood running down Garth's face as he carried me and my broken toes to the van. He turns back to his mother. "I actually feel lucky. Now that I've met you, I have everything I want. An earlobe was a small price to pay."

When it is time to leave, Wiona and Joseph hug the twins, not as tightly as the Taylors hugged Scott, but that's okay. Bart gives his sons a quick handshake. Wiona pulls us aside and says, "Officers have been over here many times since you escaped. They will continue to stop by, so be careful when you come again. I would like to take you boys back right now, but I don't think Bart is ready for that."

Ernestine nods. "I agree."

"I'll have to help him lie to the peace officers the next time they stop by. I'll try to help him understand why we have to break the rules. He'll come around. Don't give up on him. Where are you staying?"

Ernestine doesn't even hesitate. "I don't think it's safe to say at this point."

"Oh. Yeah, you're probably right."

The twins hug their mom one last time as we walk out the door. Joseph sees the mitts on the grass and tells his brothers, "Hey, you have to come back soon. We never got to play catch!"

Garth rubs Joseph's head of dirty-blonde hair affectionately. "Okay, Joseph. We'll come back soon so you can teach us to play catch."

"You don't know how?"

Jefrey scoffs, "No, no clue."

"Don't worry. I'm really good, I'll teach you. Goodbye!"

Jefrey shakes Joseph's hand. Garth pulls the little guy in for another hug. "Bye, little brother."

I sit in the front passenger seat on the ride home. I can hear the twins whispering back and forth with emotion about their family. It definitely didn't go as well as Scott's trip did, but I think we can still call this visit a success.

Chapter 12

I AM THRILLED when Mother insists that we learn how to do some landscaping, since we are pretending to be landscapers. She shows us a video on caring for plants and then outfits us in our disguises plus work gloves and boots. "How do you guys feel about wearing a jumpsuit again?" Mother asks hesitantly. "Many landscapers wear these." She holds up a plain light blue jumpsuit.

I frown. "You destroyed ours for a reason, Mom."

The scowls on my friends' faces speak for themselves.

Mother shrugs and puts the jumpsuit she's holding back into the box it came from. "Okay. That's a no to the jumpsuits."

The sun is shining, and it feels so nice on my pale flesh. Mother rubs some kind of lotion on my exposed skin, claiming I could go from white to red in one day. I am assigned a flower bed, where I'm supposed to pull out any plant that doesn't look like the three kinds of flowers that were put in there specifically. It's called weeding.

I look over at Scott, who is positively beaming as he transplants some flowers to a new flower bed for my mother. He finally gets to work with the plants he loves. I work next to Garth, who is giving up on his gloves and weeding with his bare hands. He pauses when he sees me looking at him. "Maybe I should let your father surgically separate my fingers."

"We can make gloves that will fit your fingers, Garth. Only do the surgery if you want it. The rest of us don't care."

"I care," Jefrey mutters.

"Of course, you do," Garth mutters under his breath.

"What is that supposed to mean?"

"You hate everything about me."

Jefrey sneers. "Not everything, just your ugly three-fingered hand, your obsession with Elira, how often you break the rules, the way your feet smell, the way you chew your food..."

"Got it. Thanks."

I know I'm the main reason they aren't getting along. I

feel bad and I don't want to hear the brothers fight, so I leave them and walk over to Avra to help her with her flower bed. I take off my gloves after a while just to feel the sensation of the warm, black earth. I giggle when I find a wiggly gooey-looking thing in the dirt. I pick it up to show Avra, when a man walks into the yard. I set the thing down and rush to Ernestine to point out the man. She looks at him and stands up slowly. My friends all freeze when they see the displeasure on Ernestine's face.

"Rocky, come here." He looks confused as he dusts himself off and walks over to his mother. They approach the strange balding man together. "Son, I would like you to meet your father, Frank Moore."

The man is dressed in a flannel shirt and black pants. He is slightly overweight and has straight brown hair that is balding in the front. He smiles at Rocky and says, "My boy! I always knew I'd see you again!"

Ernestine grabs Rocky and Frank by the arm and hauls them to a secluded group of trees next to the shop so they can't be overheard as easily. I sneakily follow them and work on a flower bed close by. Ernestine immediately jumps down Frank's throat. "No, you didn't think you'd see him again. You said getting him back was a lost cause. You were angry that I wouldn't give up. You left me."

The smiley man wilts before my eyes. "I always knew in my heart of hearts that you would find a way, Ernestine. I just couldn't handle the daily heartbreak that you made our life into."

Ernestine folds her arms in front of her body. "I needed love and support during the hardest time of my life, and you just left."

Frank can't raise his eyes to meet Ernestine's gaze. "It was like I had lost you both, you were never home, Ernestine. I know now that what I did was wrong." He takes a step closer to his wife. "Will you forgive me?"

"Ha!" Ernestine scoffs. Rocky glares at his mother, which softens her a little bit. "I will have to think about it."

Frank turns from Ernestine to Rocky. "I saw on the news that six people had escaped the complex, and that you were one of them. I knew when the news said that Ernestine was wanted for questioning, that she had found a way to break you out."

Rocky looks at his father silently for a minute before answering. "It was actually my friend, Elira, who figured out how to escape. Mom was waiting on the outside to help us make a getaway, and Florence has hidden us here at her house." I groan to myself. I don't care if this man is Rocky's father; Rocky shouldn't tell him too many details.

Frank nods "I went to the old house first. I walked into your study room, Ernestine. There was a map of the city of Florence sitting on your desk, and nothing else. I remembered you telling me about Florence Hamble, who lost her daughter the same day. I figured it was a sign that you were with

Florence. I looked her up and came here. Did you leave me that clue, Ernestine? Did you want me to find you? Or do you have the money and government seal of approval to leave the country?"

Ernestine can't seem to stand still. "I obviously can't ever leave the country. I—I only left you that clue because Rocky should know who his father is. That does not mean that I want you back."

Wow. The silence that follows that remark is uncomfortable. I wonder how Rocky feels as his parents talk about their mistakes and hurt feelings in front of him. My heart goes out to my friend.

He looks his father in the eye and extends his hand. His father reaches out and takes it. He then brings his other arm around for a hug. Frank Moore's eyes fill with tears. He hugs Rocky for several minutes, then lets him go.

Rocky looks at both of his parents. "Our family has been through a lot because the government took me as a toddler." Frank and Ernestine both nod in agreement. "In the complex I remembered being loved by my parents. I hated the complex after I was taken away. I was almost charged as a dissident several times because I was so angry and dissatisfied with the answers I got to my questions." Ernestine puts her arm around Rocky and squeezes him. He gives her a quick smile. "I learned to keep my mouth shut, and my head down." He looks at his dad. "Mom was miserable knowing I was alive in the complex, living my life without her. You, Dad, were miserable, seeing her miserable. I think our family needs to start over. Let's get to know each other again. If we decide we can't live together, then fine, we won't. But, maybe under happier and healthier circumstances we can. What do you say?"

Frank's wrinkled eyes crinkle deeply as he smiles. "I say yes. I would like to earn your forgiveness, Rocky. And yours, Ernestine. I would like to know my son."

Ernestine looks down at her feet. "I guess for your sake, Rocky, we can try it. I don't want him living here with us. He'll have to come visit if he is serious about entering our lives again."

Rocky nods in agreement. "Great, it's settled then. Do you have a place to stay, Dad?"

Frank looks at Ernestine wistfully. "I was hoping I could stay in our old house. It is still half mine. I could fix it up a bit. Is that okay, Ernestine?"

Father pulls into the driveway in a stylish silver car and hurries over to tell us that the authorities are patrolling the streets today and are headed this way. We start packing up our landscaping tools.

Ernestine looks both ways down the street before addressing Frank again. "It's fine, as long as you don't tell the authorities anything when they come calling. They know that's my house. I'm sure they are watching it."

"I will tell them that I just came back to town after 12

years, and I'm trying to fix up the place. You weren't there when I came back, and I don't expect you to return since you are a wanted woman."

"That's right, and don't let them trick you into giving up anything else. We are dead to you. That's what you have to say."

"Okay, Ernestine, I will."

"Good, go to it then. Don't forget the outside of the house needs a fresh coat of paint when you're done with the repairs."

Frank smiles and shakes his head. "I won't forget. Goodbye, Ernestine. Goodbye, Rocky. Your hair and your ear look good, son."

"Thanks, Dad." Frank waves at everyone, then turns and walks away.

Ernestine and I smile and wave at the passing peace officer as we load a thing called a wheelbarrow with spades and wilting weeds. I fall into step with her as she takes the wheelbarrow to the shop. "Ernestine, there are quite a few people who are in on our secret now. Does that make you nervous at all?"

"Yes, Elira, it does."

Chapter 13

THE NEXT DAY IS RAINY AND GRAY. We stay inside and try to find any information on Avra's parents that we can on the computers. We find a newspaper article with a list of parents who had signed a petition to get their children back the year we were taken.

"Did the petition change anything, Ernestine?"

"No. The petition amounted to nothing."

"At least we know that these parents want their children back."

"I know almost every name on this list. I was the one who

riled them up. I'll go check on the three names I don't know. We'll hope one of them is Avra's family."

After a four-hour jaunt outside, Ernestine returns sure that the unknown people aren't Avra's parents.

"What does that mean, Ernestine?" Avra sobs.

Ernestine wipes the tears from Avra's cheeks. "I'm guessing that your parents just aren't the type to cause trouble. They accepted the government's ruling and moved on."

"They didn't want me."

"No. Don't tell yourself that."

Avra lays her head on her arms at the kitchen table. "It feels impossible."

"Well, we aren't giving up. I will personally visit every last name on the complex's affected family list even if it takes years. You, and your parents deserve to be reunited. Fourteen years is—so long."

Avra starts sobbing again. "Th-thank you."

I wrap my arms around my best friend and let her cry on my shoulder. I meant to find her parents first, but she will be last, if we find them at all.

"Let's go in our room. I want to braid your hair."

"Okay."

She plops down in the chair at our vanity and refuses to look in the mirror. "Avra, are you okay?"

"Not really."

"How is the new medicine my dad gave you working?"

"It's fine. It works a little bit better than the complex medicine. I'm still too weak to go to visit parents though."

"I think the timing has been unlucky for you. You'll be strong on a visit day soon."

"I hope so."

"How are your cooking lessons with Freda going?"

She smiles for the first time today. "Cooking with Freda is the best. She is so nice, and we make the yummiest things ever. Did you like the three-layered brownies we made yesterday?"

"Yes. I ate three of them."

Avra laughs. "Maybe that's why we didn't get snacks in the complex. People like you can't control themselves."

I laugh too. "Yeah, probably. Don't make them so yummy next time."

"Will you paint my fingernails, Elira?"

I think longingly about Garth sitting in the great room for a second, but I want to support my friend. "Okay, choose your color."

THE NEXT DAY MOM AND DAD bring down hot cheesy sandwiches and smooth red soup for lunch. They seem really happy today. They both hug me and then each other. While they are so close they lean into each other and touch lips. All of us teenagers watch the whole exchange and sort of jump in surprise. I feel intrigued and embarrassed at the same time. It's so weird.

My dad breaks the uncomfortable silence. "What's the matter? Have you guys never seen a kiss before?"

Rocky clears his throat. "We've only seen people try to kiss through a thick plate of glass. What you just did is—different."

Scott speaks up, "My mom kissed me all over my face about 20 times when I saw her again, but she didn't kiss me here." Scott points to his lips.

Father looks at Mother and smiles. "Kissing on the lips is what you do when you love someone more than anything, and they love you back." We all nod, trusting that he knows what he is talking about.

I look at Garth, who turns to look at me at the same time. We both blush and turn away.

After lunch, Avra says she has a headache and needs to lie down. I take her into our room and tuck her in. I lie on the bed next to her hoping that she's not too tired to have a girl chat with me. "Have you kissed Scott, Avra?"

She giggles. "No. I've wanted to, but I wasn't sure how to make it happen. Your parents made it look easy."

I remember their public kiss and blush. "That was embarrassing and educational at the same time, right?"

Avra smiles at me. "How do you think your mom would react if you kissed Garth?"

"I don't know. Sometimes I think she likes him, but sometimes I think she wants to separate me from him."

"I think she knows he's a good guy. She just doesn't want to share you."

"Do you remember what she said when the peace officer was here? Do you think she secretly hates my raccoon eye?"

"She was faking it to get the officer to leave us alone."

"I hope so."

"I know so. I overheard her telling your dad that you are more beautiful and smart than she imagined you would be."

"Really?"

"Yes. She's the kind of mom everyone should have."

I look at the picture of my mom and me hugging cheek to cheek on the wall and sigh. "She really does love me just the way I am, doesn't she?"

"Of course she does, Elira."

"I always felt like I was one of the lucky ones in the complex. Now I know I'm lucky."

Avra sighs as she looks at the same picture on the wall. "I hope my mom is just like her."

"Do you remember your parents at all, Avra?"

She twirls a piece of hair around her finger thoughtfully. "When I try to remember my earliest memory, I swear I remember smiling brown faces and a train whistle."

"A train whistle? Do you remember them taking you on a train?"

"No, I never got on the train, even though I wanted to. I just heard the train whistle all the time. Several times a day."

Why didn't she mention this before? "Uh, that's huge, Avra. You should have told me sooner. We need to check out all the neighborhoods along the train tracks."

She sits up in bed. "Oh, yeah. We should. Well, you can. They are never going to let me go outside, are they?"

"Avra, how do you feel about your health? If you think you can handle going outside, I'll insist that we take you the next time we go out."

"I want to, it's just that outside air is cold and hurts my lungs when I breathe in too hard."

I tap my fingers together thoughtfully. "We won't be chased again, hopefully. That should help keep your breathing even. We could drive a car along the train tracks and look for Avra look-alikes the next time we go out. It would be helpful to have you with us, even if you just stay in the car."

She perks up. "Okay, I think I can do that."

"Good."

"Do you remember what your house looked like, by chance?"

She scrunches her eyebrows together as she thinks. "I know this sounds weird, but I think it was bright yellow."

"Why do you think that?"

"I just have memories with bright yellow in the background."

"The inside of your house might have been bright yellow, though."

She shrugs. "Yeah, maybe."

I am relieved to have a new angle to find her parents. "I will knock on every door along the railroad track till I find them for you."

She grins and claps her hands. "Good. We finally have a plan."

"This is a good day." I grab the sweet-smelling lotion on the bedside table and rub some into my dry hands. "How are things between you and Scott, by the way?"

Avra raises her eyebrows. "Good enough. He is really focused on his family right now. I understand why. I just feel left out sometimes. I'm the only one who hasn't met their parents yet, you know."

I feel terrible. I've been so selfish. "I'm sorry I haven't been sensitive to your feelings, Avra."

"I'm fine. Don't worry about it. Scott just seemed so into me; now he's completely focused on his family. I don't want to be forgotten. How are you and the twins?"

I smile at my hands. "Uh, it's not even a choice anymore. Garth is the one that makes me happy."

"Have things changed since he met his family?"

I nod as I think about it. "It's about the same for us as it is for you and Scott. He is excited and focused on his family right now. But occasionally he does something for me, and looks at me with those clear blue eyes, and I just melt."

"How's Jefrey?"

I shrug indifferently. "I think he has some major issues. He was not nice to his parents the first time he saw them. They had to be in shock; you have to give people time to process things, you know."

"Does he still like you?"

"Supposedly. I am not giving him any encouragement though."

"He seems obsessed with money. I see him eyeing the money anytime your mom gives some to Ernestine."

"Yeah, I've noticed that too. We've never needed money before. I don't know why he is so interested in it."

"Was his parents' house like this one?"

"No, it was nice, but it was much smaller."

"Maybe he thinks that you won't like him unless he has as much as you have."

"That's dumb. Nobody can have exactly the same amount as anyone else. Having a bigger house or more cars doesn't make you a better person."

Avra looks at me with sad eyes and nods. "I know, but I worry that my parents will have the least of all of them. I don't want you guys to stop being my friends."

I stop and look at my best friend. "I thought we were talking about Jefrey."

She looks at her hands. "I—we are talking about Jefrey."

I reach out and take her hand. "Even if you have nothing and no family, you will always be my friend."

Avra's brown eyes look deeply into mine. "Thank you."

"You're welcome; get some sleep."

I walk to the door and slip out quietly. I don't see Garth standing there, and he startles me. "Ah! Garth."

He looks around and sees no one near us. He wraps his arms around me, which brings me so close to him, I can almost feel his heart beating. I hug him back. My heartbeat quickens with how good he feels in my arms. Then his face that is so close slowly starts to get closer. Is he going to—kiss me? I just wait, hoping he will. My eyes close as I feel his breath tickling my nose. He kisses my cheek. That's getting closer, will he make it all the way to my...

"HEY!" Jefrey comes charging up to us. "What do you two think you're doing?"

"This is none of your business, Jef." Garth says as he pushes his brother away from us.

"I think it is. I have just as much of a relationship with Elira as you have."

"Is that true, Elira?" Garth asks.

I see pain in both of the faces staring at me. "No, it's not. I'm sorry, Jefrey."

Jefrey shakes his head. "I'm not giving up."

"I've tried to give you a chance, Jefrey, but I just don't

feel the same for you anymore. I'm sorry. I've made my choice and I choose Garth." I stand up on my tippy toes and give Garth the kiss I wanted him to give me. I meant to be quick, so I could hide from these two in my room, but, wow. I feel like something just awoke in me, and I can't be quick about it. When I pull away from Garth, I can see he feels the same way by the dazed look in his eyes. Our moment is quickly squashed by Jefrey punching a hole in the wall. I look into Garth's perfect eyes one last time before I run into my room and collapse against the door.

Bam. Smack. "You are no brother of mine!"

"She's the one who chose. Don't blame me."

I scoot to the side of the door as I hear the brothers fighting, physically and verbally. I'm pretty sure Jefrey threw a punch at Garth, then Garth wrestled Jefrey to the floor. The walls and the door keep getting kicked and bashed into. What have I done? I just wanted Garth to know that I wanted to kiss him, and I wanted Jefrey to know that he had no chance, so he could get over it. Now they are out there beating each other up. I can hear every word of their fight.

"You always get everything I want. Why are you so special, Garth?"

"I'm not that special, but I'm a better choice than you!"

"You have a messed-up hand, and a messed-up ear. She must like ugly jerks."

"You are messed-up too. Inside and out, so shut up!"

148

Should I go out there and stop them? I feel like I will just make it worse or maybe I'm just a chicken. Either way, I just stay put.

"I was the first one to ever talk to her at the complex. She fell for me, hard. I could tell."

"Well, even if she fell for you first, your whiny baby-ness changed her mind."

"This whiny baby just put a fist in your face." The rustling sounds stop.

"Yeah, you did. Nice hook. Look, Jefrey, she chose me. That sucks for you, but can you get over it? We are brothers still."

"That's what you think." *Bam.* It sounds like Jefrey hits the wall one last time and storms off.

I feel tears forming in my eyes, but I do everything I can to keep them from falling. I am the reason that fight just happened. I thought if I made my choice known everything would get better between them. Now it's ten times worse.

I force myself to my feet and turn the doorknob. I gasp as I see Garth doubled over holding his side. He has a black eye and probably bruised ribs. I rush to his side and wrap my arms around him.

"Ow. Not so tight on my right side."

"I'm sorry. I shouldn't have kissed you in front of him. I'm such an idiot."

"Don't ever say that." Then he kisses me, and we can take as long as we want this time.

Chapter 14

THE TWINS LOOK BAD TODAY. Garth's eye is black as night, and Jefrey has a fat lip. They are told off by Ernestine and Mom at breakfast for fighting and damaging the walls in the hall.

"What do you have to say for yourselves?" Mother asks.

"Sorry for the holes in the walls, but he deserved it," Jefrey insists.

Garth rolls his eyes at Jefrey. "We'll fix the damage we caused, Mrs. Hamble. It won't happen again."

"Would you like to tell me what it was about?"

The twins glance briefly at me then glare at each other. "No," Jefrey insists.

Garth looks pleadingly at my mother. "It's not something we want to talk about, but it won't be repeated."

"It better not. Elira has a plan to find Avra's parents. Ernestine will be taking the girls out today, but you two will have to stay here and patch the walls."

"Mom, I'm not sure the two of them should..."

"I think the girls and the boys in this house should have some time away from each other."

"But they might..."

"I won't budge on this, Elira. You and Avra get your disguises on. It's time to go."

"Okay, Mother." I bite my lip as I pass the twins with Avra by my side. Garth steals a glance at me before my mother notices.

Avra touches the two holes in the wall before we enter our room. "Did I really sleep through all that?"

I sigh. "Yes, you did."

"It was over you, wasn't it?"

"Yeah. I thought it was time to let Jefrey know that I have made my choice. So I kissed Garth right in front of him."

Avra laughs. "You did what? Ha! It all makes sense now."

I hide my face in my hand. "They hate each other. I really don't want them to kill each other while we're gone."

"That would be a shame. You'd have no one to kiss anymore."

I blush as I remember kissing Garth. "Yeah, that would be a shame."

I squeeze Garth's hand as we walk down the hall in our disguises. I want to hug him, but my mom glares at us, and I don't dare. Scott gets to come with us so we can drop him off at his parents' house for his 12:00 meeting.

Avra smiles as we pull up to the Taylors' house. Scott's little sisters are waiting by the gate. Scott jumps out of the car and whispers something to the little girls. They smile and wave at Avra. She giggles and waves back.

"Why didn't you tell me his sisters were so cute, Elira?"

"I thought I did."

"Well, maybe you did, but wow. I'm in love with them; they're so little." We pull away from the Taylors' house and head to the other side of town by the railroad tracks. Avra seems to feel pretty good. She is awake and attentive as we pull into the first neighborhood by the railroad tracks. The houses are midsized and older, but they are mostly kept-up and respectable looking. Ernestine parks the car and asks Avra if she is ready to go door to door. She shakes her head, "Is it okay if I watch you two do it for a while? I just want to stay in the car for now."

"Okay—Elira, you get the right side of the road, I will get the left. Remember, just ask them if they have seen your lost dog. People are pretty friendly if they know you aren't selling anything," Ernestine tells me.

"Got it, let's go."

I walk to the first house. It's not yellow, so I don't have high hopes. *Knock, knock.* A chubby blonde woman with a blonde baby on her hip answers the door. I smile sweetly at her. "Hello, have you seen a dog wandering loose around here? Mine has gone missing."

"Yeah, I saw a big black one trotting down the road earlier."

"Oh, mine is small and brown. Thanks anyway."

"No problem."

I continue down the road. No one looks anything like Avra. I see a yellow house coming up, and I am sure I'll find her parents there. When I get to the yellow house, I take a deep breath and knock on the door. A red-headed man covered in freckles opens the door. My heart sinks. I say my dog speech, then I ask, "Do you live here alone? I was wondering if this was a good neighborhood for families. My older brother is wanting to relocate."

"Uh, my wife and I live here. It's all right."

"What does she look like? I mean, I just passed a brunette jogger a few minutes ago. Was that her?" I say, scrambling to think of a good excuse for my curiosity.

"My wife ain't brunette. She's a blonde, and she don't jog. She's working at the gas station all day."

"Oh, thank you for your help. Have a nice day."

He grunts at me as he shuts the door. I go on to the next house, and the next, and the next. No luck. I walk back to the car dejectedly. Ernestine is already done with her side of the road. She says there was only one possibility on her side of the road, but after some careful questioning, she doesn't think they are Avra's parents. We drive to the next neighborhood. The houses are much smaller, and the yards are weedy and run down.

Ernestine takes a big drink from a water bottle. "Okay, Avra. Are you ready to talk to people?"

"Uh, I guess I could do one or two houses by the car."

"Well, that's a start. Let's go."

I watch out the corner of my eye as Avra approaches the house next to mine. The woman who answers has white-blonde hair and pale white skin, so it's probably not her family. I see that the last house on my side of the road is a yellow one. I am not too enthusiastic until I get to that one. Avra is back in the car. She could only do two houses before she was too tired. At least that's what she claimed. I wonder if she's kind of scared of meeting her parents, despite her eagerness. I approach the yellow house and give the door a good hard knock. A man with light brown skin answers. My heart starts pounding like crazy. I do my dog speech. The man scratches his head and says he hasn't seen any dogs wandering around.

"My brother and his family are looking at a house for sale

in this neighborhood. Do you think it's a good neighborhood for families?"

"It's okay, but there aren't a lot of kids around here."

"Do you have children?"

"No. I don't have any children, or a wife, or any relatives. Sorry, I'm not much help. You may want to ask the house across the street. They have kids."

"Oh, okay. Thank you, have a nice day."

I trudge slowly back to the car. I was so sure he was Avra's dad. I guess not. Ernestine beats me back again. She had two possibilities on her side of the road, but she was pretty sure they weren't Avra's family. We write down my yellow house's address and Ernestine's two possible addresses, just in case.

We go to a drive-through restaurant for lunch. It feels like we are talking to someone on the telephone when we order our food. A minute later I look out the car window to see the lady who talked to us through the machine. She hands us a bag of hamburgers and fries and tells us to have a nice day. I think I will have a nice day. That was awesome.

After lunch we drive to the last neighborhood by the train tracks in town. If we don't find her family here, we'll have to drive to the next town and try again. Avra and I are going to start at opposite ends of the right-hand side of the street and meet in the middle. I'm pleased to see that there are many yellow houses on this street. I'm not pleased to see that the houses are tiny and run down—every one of them.

I start on the far end, giving my lost dog speech. I don't meet any possibilities for a while. Avra is only five houses away, and Ernestine is almost right across the street when a man pulls up to a yellow house two down from me in a shabby looking blue sedan with a red hood and a white door. He climbs out and struggles to get the door to shut properly. His chocolatey brown skin piques my interest, but when he looks at me, I swear I'm looking at an older, male version of Avra. He tips his dirty, wide-brimmed black hat at me as he walks into his house. I wave at Avra and Ernestine to join me.

I grab Avra by the shoulders. "I'm sure that was your father! He looks just like you. We need to do this together." She nods nervously. "We don't need to do the dog approach. Just cut to the chase." We approach the yellow house; I insist that Avra knocks. She shivers and shakes as the door opens. The man looks at us all briefly, then focuses on Avra. I nudge her.

She finds the courage to speak. "I—I was wondering if you had a d-daughter named Avra years ago."

The man doesn't say anything for a long time, then he opens the door wider and says, "Why don't you come in a minute?"

We all nod and enter the small, raggedy-looking house. There is one couch with stuffing coming out of the arms. The three of us sit on that. It feels like our backsides hit the floor, but we try not to look startled. The man walks over to a small, scratched wooden table, picks up a familiar-looking newspaper

157

on the seat of a hard, wooden chair and tosses it onto the table. He puts the chair in front of the couch and sits on it.

The man looks into Avra's eyes and says, "Yes, I had a daughter named Avra. She had a bad heart and the government took her away when she was two."

Avra folds her shaking hands together and says, "I—I am Avra. I just broke out of the complex."

The man nods his head as he looks at her. "Peace officers have visited here a few times looking for you." His eyes keep flitting over to the discarded newspaper on the table. "You, uh, look like me. Your mother always wished that you looked more like her."

"Where is my mother?"

"She is at work. She leaves for the sock factory at six in the morning, and she gets home at six at night."

"Do I have any brothers or sisters?"

"You have a sister, Roselle, but she stays at your aunt's and your grandma's house a lot. She's fourteen. I wish I had a picture to show you, but I don't have any."

Avra looks around the blank, dirty walls hungrily. "Can I meet my sister and my mother?"

"Yes, but not tonight. Tonight is a bad night in this neighborhood. Come back in four days. Come at 6:00, when your mom gets off work, bring all your friends so I can meet them. It must have been hard escaping the complex. I want to hear all about it when your mother and your sister are here."

He stands up, so we get up too. "Okay, we'll come back in four days," Avra says.

Ernestine looks the man in the eye. "Please don't tell anyone else about our meeting. We have to live in hiding. We are wanted people now."

"Yes, I know."

"What is your name, sir?"

"Jim Brown."

Avra approaches her dad, hoping for a hug. They awkwardly reach out and hug each other but let go quickly. We walk silently to the door, unsure of what to say when Jim says, "See you in a few days," then sends us out the door and shuts it.

I look at Ernestine and she looks quizzically at me. That was a really weird visit. We look at Avra, who is soaking in her surroundings with a mixture of happiness and pain on her face. The corners of her mouth turn up when she says, "I found my family. I can't wait to meet my mother and sister. Let's go home so I can tell Scott."

I give her hand a squeeze. "Okay. He will be so happy for you."

Avra looks out the window the whole ride home. When we get to my parents' house, she rushes in and finds Scott sitting at the table. "Scott, I found my family! I have a father, a mother, and a sister named Roselle. Only my dad was home today. I get to meet all of them in four days."

"That's great, Avra!" He hugs her and laughs with her.

I feel like something is off. Something is off about Avra's dad, and something is off about her reaction. I can't put my finger on it though. When Avra goes to bed early, I approach Ernestine and my mom in the kitchen.

"Ernestine, what do you think about Avra's dad?"

Ernestine frowns and scratches her head. "I think he lives in poverty, and he may have been happy to have one less mouth to feed when Avra was taken away."

"Really?"

"Yes. Did you see the empty cupboards? That's probably why the sister stays with relatives so much."

I look at the wall that is shared between the basement kitchen and our bedroom. I imagine my sweet friend curled up on the cloud-like bed behind the wall. "Can we trust him? We do have a $100,000 bounty on our heads."

Ernestine twists her lips together. "That's a good question. I wish I knew the answer."

Mother looks at Ernestine with worry in her eyes and shrugs. "If we don't let her go to her family, it'll break her heart. I don't know if I can deny her what she wants so badly."

Ernestine nods in agreement. "We have to decide between what the heart wants and what the brain says is logical."

I'M RELIEVED that the twins did not kill each other

while I was gone. The holes in the wall are patched. Garth approaches my mom after dinner and says yet again, "Mrs. Hamble, I'd just like to say how sorry I am again about your walls. I'll paint them when the patches are dry."

"I accept your apology. You've had a long day; you should go to bed." Mother stands with her arms folded as Garth hugs me good night. I sigh with disappointment. I guess a gentle hug is all I'm going to get tonight.

I whisper in his ear, "Is Jefrey going to be all right?"

"Yeah. Don't worry about him."

"Okay. Should I be worried about you?"

"Only if it means I'll get longer hugs—and kisses"

My cheeks immediately turn red. I let go of Garth and walk to my bedroom door. Mother frowns at me when she sees my smile and the blush on my cheeks as I close the door to my room.

When I crawl into bed, I assume Avra is asleep, but the sniffling I hear tells me I'm wrong.

"My parents are poor, Elira," Avra says through the covers.

"Can you breathe under there?"

She glares at me. "Yes, I can breathe, but I didn't see any food or anything, really, in my parents' house."

"It's okay to be poor. I used to think that all parents were poor outside the complex. Their food was probably in the fridge."

Avra pulls the covers away from her mouth so I can hear

her better. "I think you have more in this one bedroom, than my parents have in their entire house."

I look around our room and have to agree with her. "That doesn't bother me. Does it bother you?"

She covers her eyes with her hand. "I feel sad and embarrassed. My dad said to bring all my friends, but I don't want everyone to see how poor they are."

"I understand. You don't have to bring everyone if you don't want to. In fact, I don't think we should go with you. The bounty is too tempting to risk it."

"It wasn't too risky for you to go with Scott or the twins."

"I—I know. It's just that people in that neighborhood would have so much to gain with $100,000. Don't be mad."

"I'm not. I understand." Avra almost convinces me except for the tear that is sliding down her cheek.

It's time to bring up the positive things about today. "I bet you want to meet your mom and sister, right?"

Her eyes light up. "Yes, I do. Do you think my sister looks like me?"

"I hope so, because you are breathtakingly beautiful."

"Why do you always say that?"

"Because it's true, and I guess my raccoon eye and I are a little bit jealous."

Avra laughs. "I can't believe that you could be jealous of anything that I have."

"Well, believe it, sister."

"Thanks for being my friend, Elira."

"Thanks for being mine, too."

Chapter 15

I HAVE AN UNEASY FEELING all day long. I pretend
to be happy when Garth and Jefrey have a successful visit
to their parents without killing each other. I didn't go with
them this time. I want those two to be on their best behavior
in front of their dad, and I'm afraid that I don't bring out the
best in them right now. Scott had a great visit with his parents
yesterday, and he goes back again today. He is lucky that they
live so close, and that they miss and love him so much. Rocky
is finally feeling better, and he wants to help his dad do some

work on their house. Ernestine doesn't want him to go alone, so she goes with him.

My mom, Avra, and I, have a nice morning painting each other's fingernails with tiny little bottles of paint and tiny paintbrushes. It is fun to have some "girl time," as my mother calls it. Avra doesn't seem to think so though. She breaks down in tears as we finish and rushes to our room.

"Mom, I don't know what to do for her."

"You are doing all you can. Some battles have to be fought alone, especially inner battles."

Knock, knock. I rush to the bookcase and pull out the red book. I shut myself into the hidden room as quick as a wink.

I hear a woman's voice through the door. She sounds friendly and familiar. The hidden door opens up and my mother stands there alone looking at me uncertainly. "I let the woman who claims to be Maxine in and I have taken her upstairs. I hope this isn't a set-up."

"What? Maxine is here?" I run up the stairs as quickly as I can without looking back.

"Maxine!" My favorite mentor, my surrogate mother greets me in the doorway of the piano room. I wrap my arms around her and squeeze her as tight as I can.

Maxine looks five years older, but she is happy to see me. "Elira, I'm so glad you're safe."

"Maxine, I am so happy to see you!"

My mother clears her throat. "I let her in because she said she met Ernestine at her house. Ernestine sent her over."

"I'm so glad Ernestine was at her house when you called. Maxine, this is my mother, Florence Hamble."

Maxine turns to my mother and extends her hand. "I have known of you for some time, but it is nice to meet you personally, Florence."

My mother is still skeptical for some reason as she takes Maxine's hand. "How do you know of me?"

"Your husband does extraordinary work in the medical field, and I know he has a generous heart for those who can't pay for all of his services. I know you do much for the poor and hungry of Herrington as well. Your kind reputation has preceded you."

Mother finally softens up. "Oh, well, thank you. I have heard many great things about you as well, Maxine. Elira said you helped her escape, and that you were the one kind adult she could turn to in that place."

Maxine's eyes fill with sadness. "I certainly tried. Do you mind if we sit down? There is much going on in the complex lately that you should know about."

"Yes, have a seat, and I will get us some cold ginger ale."

I sit down across from Maxine and try not to explode with questions. "What is going on in the complex? Is Shasta okay? Was she punished for helping me?"

She takes my hand like she is afraid of what my reaction

will be. "Shasta is okay, but she was interrogated. She told them that you wanted to escape to save Avra's life. They asked her why the specific boys went with you, but she didn't know. She was a mess when they finished with her. She is being fed medicated food. Actually, all residents of the complex are being medicated from age 10 and up now."

My stomach turns and I feel like I am going to throw up. Poor Shasta. It's all my fault. "Why are they medicating them all? And so early?"

Maxine shakes her head in disgust. "The complex chief was livid when you escaped. He ordered the medication in the food to be changed to a new mix of hormonal inhibitors and behavior modification drugs. He is afraid that people are going to escape more, now that you've been successful."

"Oh, no. I didn't think about what would happen to the friends I left behind." I bury my head in my hands.

She pats my knee. "It's worse for the residents but I feel a shift happening with the mentors and other employees. They know in their hearts that what is happening in there is inhumane and just plain wrong. It's good to not be the only one who resents it now."

I look up from my hands. "What about you? Were you punished?"

Mother returns and gives us each a glass of ice-cold ginger ale.

Maxine sits back in her chair and shrugs. "I was

interrogated, but so was every other mentor at the complex. I chose my words well."

"Mentors aren't tortured though, right?"

She takes a long drink of ginger ale. "Correct. I just sat in a chair with my rights intact."

I think of the other mentors at the complex. "Did Mentor Bridget or Mentor Roberta tell the chief that you had a connection to me?"

Maxine wrinkles her nose and nods. "Roberta did mention it, unfortunately. I wasn't there when you escaped, so I think that was my saving grace." Mother smiles in relief. "The Complex Chief thinks the patient rights I have suggested over the years contributed to your escape." She shrugs. "I was basically demoted and have been reassigned to the five-year old girls and any other grunt job that they can find. I have been very formal and careful since you left."

My mother looks at Maxine curiously. "What made you want to be a mentor in the complex? Have you always been against the complex system?"

Maxine's eyes look sad for a moment. "I had a sister who was four years younger than me. Her birthday was January 15th, so she didn't have her mandatory check-up until she was almost three. I was seven at the time. My mother was hopeful that they wouldn't notice that she was blind. Unfortunately, they did notice, and they took her away. I was determined from that point on that I would get a job in the complex one day so I could see my sister again."

I sit on the edge of my seat, enthralled by Maxine's story. "So, did you see her again?"

"Even though I applied every year after I reached adulthood, I didn't get the job at the complex until I was thirty."

"So, your sister was 26."

"Yes. They had her working in the laundry room, folding sheets and pillowcases day after day, for eight years. I was thrilled when I finally found her down there."

"Was she happy to see you? Or, not see you? Feel you, again?"

"She didn't remember me at first. I found every excuse to go down to the laundry room for weeks. She would talk to me, but she didn't believe I was her sister until one day someone accidentally tripped me when I was walking toward her. She heard my scream and jolted out of her chair. She said she remembered that scream when she was taken away from her family. She finally believed I was her sister."

"Was? Is she dead?"

She frowns as she looks into her glass. "Yes. She accidentally tripped on the cords of several hot irons and burned herself severely. No one hurried to her aid. An infection set in, and within three weeks—she died." Maxine wipes a single tear from her eye with a finger.

Mother shakes her head. "My cook, Freda, suffered from severe burns, but she didn't get an infection."

"I don't think the doctors did much for her. She was blind and now covered in burns, so they just let the infection take her."

I feel a tear forming in my eye as I watch Maxine's face crumple. "What was her name?"

"Cheri."

"What a beautiful name."

"After I finally found out where they had taken her, I watched her die of the infection. I decided from that moment that I would help anyone in the complex who needed my help. I felt a connection to you, Elira, from the beginning. I am so proud of you for getting so many people out."

The appreciation that I've always had for Maxine doubles somehow. "Thank you for telling me about Cheri. That must have been horrible. I'm so glad you're okay. I've been worried about you and Shasta."

Maxine's eyes darken. "You are right to be worried, Elira. Things were never good there, but they are so much worse for the residents now. They are creating mindless zombies who just eat, sleep, and work."

"What about their schooling?"

"They've cut schooling hours in half for age 10 and up and are starting them at jobs for the second half of the day. They are all so medicated that they don't fight back. It's disgusting. All the things I fought for all these years have been undone. I told them that starting them working too early would cut their life spans in half. I guess they don't care anymore and unfortunately, I'm not in a position to help anyone who is getting over-worked.

I shake my head in frustration. "I bet the dissident levels have dropped since they started medicating everyone."

"Yeah, dissidents are nonexistent now."

"Speaking of dissidents, I've been wondering since I escaped... What happened to Andric?"

Maxine swirls her ginger ale around the ice cubes in her glass. "He was medicated with the original concoction, but it did no good. He'd been in trouble a lot the last couple of years. They—took him to the final doctor."

"So he really is dead." I feel the pain of seeing him taken away all over again. "What does the final doctor do to kill them?"

Maxine clears her throat. "He gives them a lethal injection, and they don't wake up. They are buried on the hill without a headstone."

I set my glass down on the coffee table with a loud *thump*. "Mom, are you hearing this? What can we do?" Mom looks to Maxine for help.

Maxine sighs. "I don't know how, but if I could, I would get all residents out of the complex in the next couple years. Those ten-year-olds aren't going to make it to thirty in my opinion. We've lost five of them already to the machines."

I gasp in surprise. "Maxine, children are dying trying to do adult work."

She nods. "They aren't mentally or physically ready; it's outrageous."

I imagine this basement filled with my friends from the complex. "Even if we did get everyone out, how can we hide that many people with deformities?"

My mother joins in, "We can't hide that many. We have to change the government's policies so they can go home to their parents. Not all, but, most parents will want them back, I think."

I like the sound of that but... "How can we do that, Mom?"

Mother taps a finger on her chin as she thinks. "Maxine, do you think you could hide a little camera on you somewhere when you are in the complex, and record what they are doing to those people?"

"I am with the five-year-olds now. I can record them pretty easily, but the worst things to see are happening with the ten-year-olds and up."

Mother taps her fingers together. "Could you switch shifts with someone in the older groups for a day?"

"Now that you mention it, I actually did arrange to cover a shift for Roberta on National Purification Day before the escape happened."

I cringe as I think of Mentor Roberta. I have no idea what National Purification Day is, but it sounds like something I probably wouldn't like. "Perfect."

Mother claps her hands. "We will get as much video footage as we can. I know someone who works at the national news station. I can convince him to put it on air without telling his boss."

"Who do you know, Mom?"

"Greggory just got a job there."

I laugh out loud until I see my mom frowning at me. "Are you sure he'll do it?"

"He'll do anything for a bribe."

I'm not so sure my selfish, lazy brother will do anything for me or anyone else. I'm actually surprised to hear he has a job. "Did you get him that job?"

Mother looks at me with reproach. "No, he actually applied for it all on his own."

"Huh. That's surprising."

"It really is, but I think we should use this opportunity while we have it."

Maxine takes a long drink of ginger ale. "That will get people stirred up and talking for sure, but I think we will need a politician on our side to actually get the law changed."

Mother smiles. "I know someone in politics who might just help us."

Chapter 16

MY BROTHERS ARE ON MY MIND this morning. They seemed like self-serving jerks when I met them. We could really use their help, but I'm not sure they have the best interest of myself and others like me at heart. My mom is sure they will help. Well, we're about to find out. They are coming here for a meeting tonight.

I tell my friends about Maxine's visit and my mother's plan over lunch. Rocky and Garth are completely for it. Avra and Scott say they'll do whatever the rest of us decide. Jefrey won't look me in the eye. He's been like this since I kissed Garth in front of him. He looks at me long enough to say, "It won't work. The people are happy without people like us out here."

I glower at him. "Where is your evidence for that? We don't talk to enough people to know how they feel."

"My dad had two kids taken to the complex and he still thinks it's the best thing for the country."

I huff. "He listens to the wrong people. The video of the complex with their medicated food, interrogations, and death doctor will change his mind. I know this is a good plan."

Jefrey mutters under his breath as he leaves the table, "You wouldn't know a good thing if you saw it." I'm angry more than sad as I watch him walk away.

Garth brings me back to the issue at hand. "The truth is, people don't know what goes on in there. Some of them may have agreed with the complex life that we had, but what they are doing now is totally different. It's inhuman."

Rocky looks at me before speaking. "Your brothers have never had to suffer. If you bring the suffering and injustice that Shasta and Bryon are living to light, they'll feel something. They'll want to help us."

"I hope so, Rocky."

I MAKE SURE I'M DRESSED like a strong independent woman before I walk upstairs for the meeting with my brothers. I don't cover my raccoon eye with makeup. I want my brothers to see the brain behind the blemish. When Brock and Greggory's skeptical stares hit me, I have to think of Shasta and everyone else in the complex mindlessly working like zombies.

"Are you going to be up there all night?" Garth asks from behind me as he sees me hesitating at the bottom of the stairs.

I don't turn around. I just look up the stairs. "Probably." I let out a long breath. "My brothers don't believe in our cause, but I need to convert them to it. I just don't think they respect me enough to care what I say."

Garth wraps his arms around me from behind. I let myself sink into him. He whispers in my ear, "Just be yourself. They will want to join your cause, just like I did in the complex."

How does he know what I need to hear? I turn around to say, "Thank you, Gar—" He stops my mouth with a kiss. I hear a door slam in the hall. I guess Jefrey saw that.

"A-hem. It's time to meet your brothers in the dining room, sweetheart." Mother doesn't look at Garth as she links arms with me and takes me upstairs. We walk in silence for a minute.

"Mom, do you like Garth?"

"Yes."

"Are you upset that he kissed me?"

"Mmm. Well, I think you are entitled to kiss a boy at your

age, but you are both very young and you live in the same house. Please don't try to grow up too fast."

"I won't, Mom."

Greggory arrives first. He has shaved since the last time we met, and his clothes are clean. It suits him. He sits down at the dining room table and looks at Mother contemptuously. "If you want me to help thousands of deformed people that I don't know, the least you can do is let me meet the deformed people living in my parents' basement. I say we have this meeting downstairs."

Mother looks at me questioningly. I raise my eyebrows at her. I actually like that idea. It kind of feels like we have an upstairs company versus downstairs company unspoken rule going on. I know we're in hiding, but those who know our secret should learn to mingle with us. "Okay, Greggory. Let's move this meeting downstairs. I'm sure my friends won't mind."

Greggory nods his approval but lets me lead the way down the stairs. He cautiously walks behind me into our safe house. He pauses at the bottom of the stairs and looks around. His eyes linger on my friends sitting around the chess board. I sit down at the table and smile at him as I pat the seat next to me. Mother appears a minute later and squeezes past Greggory to place some delicious-looking cookies and pastries on the table. They are probably to butter my brothers up.

Greggory walks toward me, but is intercepted by Rocky,

who takes my brother's hand and shakes it. "You must be Greggory. I am Rocky. Elira has told me all about you. She is a strong leader and so are your parents. I appreciate how much they've done for my mother and for me. Thank you for caring about the friends we left behind." Greggory's eyes don't leave the side of Rocky's face with the missing ear.

All of my friends have been informed how important it is to get my brothers on our side. I'm grateful for their help. Garth rushes over to shake Greggory's hand next. "Greggory, it's nice to meet you. Any relative of Elira's will always be respected by me. She is—the most amazing person I have ever met. I truly appreciate you being brave enough to stand up for people who can't stand up for themselves." Greggory nods at Garth wordlessly.

Jefrey sulks into the room and watches what is going on from the computer desk. Scott and Avra slowly walk over and introduce themselves. "Hello, I'm Scott. Thank you for helping us."

Greggory finally finds his voice. "I haven't exactly agr..."

"Hi, I'm Avra. Your sister's best friend. She saved my life and I would do anything for her. I hope you know how lucky you are to have a sister like her."

Greggory seems perplexed that he is getting so much attention. "I guess she's..." Avra is having a bad health day, and her knees give out after she shakes Greggory's hand. Scott has one arm supporting her but Greggory gets behind Avra and lets her fall into him as she sinks to the floor.

Greggory looks stunned to be sitting on the floor with Avra on his lap. She turns her head around so their faces are super close. "I'm so sorry. Thank you for breaking my fall."

Greggory looks at her intently but doesn't say anything until he and Scott get Avra to her feet. "Are—are you okay, Avra?"

Avra wipes her tousled hair out of her face. "Yeah, this happens at least once a month. I just hope I didn't hurt you."

"Oh, no. No harm done." He continues to look concerned as he helps Scott move her to the sofa. He lets go of her hand much slower than I would expect him to. Greggory then sits next to me at the table and stuffs a cherry turnover in his mouth.

Between bites he whispers to me, "I have never seen someone do that before."

I whisper back, "She has good days and bad days. Today is a bad day."

Greggory looks at the back of Avra's head on the sofa and stuffs a cookie in his mouth. "I feel so bad for her, which is weird for me." Greggory stuffs a third treat in his mouth. "Maybe shutting all the sick people away keeps our hearts from feeling the way they should."

"Maybe," I whisper back.

Rocky approaches the table like he wants to join our

conversation, but I shake my head at him. I want to talk to my brother alone for a few minutes. Greggory's green eyes look down at Rocky's retreating back and then at me as he says, "I wanted to tell you thank you for giving my flask back the other day. Mom and Dad wouldn't have done that."

I nod in agreement. Dad especially would be furious if he knew I'd given it back. "I know, but you are old enough to make your own choices, good or bad."

Greggory sits a little taller. "Yeah, I am." His eyes meet mine. "You are old enough to make tough choices too. I haven't been able to get your story about breaking your toes to escape out of my head." I look down at my mostly-healed toes, grateful the story he's thinking about is in the past. He looks at my toes too and says, "I realized that you have made an impact on people's lives already at your young age, and I really haven't done anything except piss my family off my whole life."

"I'm sure you've done more than that."

Greggory pauses to think for a few seconds. "No, not really."

I try to hide my smile. "I hear you have a job now."

"Yep, I received my first paycheck for my own work yesterday." He pulls a check out of his pocket and unfolds it for me to see. His finger traces his name on the check.

"That's great, Greggory. How do you feel? Proud?"

He nods as he looks at the check. "I haven't cashed it yet,

because I love seeing my name on it, and knowing it's money that wasn't just given to me. I earned this."

"What's the difference?"

Greggory pauses again. "It's completely different."

"I thought money was money."

"Mom and Dad didn't hand me this check or get me this job. I decided to turn in the application. I did the interview, and somehow my boss likes me." Greggory shakes his head as if he can't believe it. "I've only been there three weeks and Mr. Fronze already trusts me with the key to the vault."

That surprises me. "Wow, should he? Are you tempted to steal from him?"

Greggory's eyes sweep around the room to see if anyone is close enough to hear us. "I was at first, but the way he looks at me made me change my mind."

"The way he looks at you?"

"Yeah. When Dad looks at me, I see skepticism, disappointment, and distrust in his eyes. When Mr. Fronze looks at me, I see respect and trust."

I can't believe Mr. Fronze is taking this leap of faith with my brother, but I'm grateful. His respect is changing Greggory.

Brock's entrance interrupts us as he is escorted down the stairs by my father. He gets a royal welcome from my friends too. Greggory slips the check back in his pocket before anyone else can ask about it.

I observe Brock's reaction to my friends, who go out of

their way to thank Brock for helping them. He seems mildly touched, but still wary about this whole thing.

When everyone except Avra is sitting around the table, my father stands up to speak to us. "Welcome to our first ever complex revolution meeting. The first thing I would like to do, is congratulate Brock and his wife Chantilly on the exciting news that they will be having a little boy in a few months!" We all clap and congratulate Brock, who seems moderately happy for the attention, but also seems bothered about something.

"Father, you know that I am just here to hear what you have to say. I am in no way pledging my allegiance to a cause that will ruin my political career."

"I understand, son, but I think in time, you'll see that at least half of the population is against the complex system."

"Why aren't they vocal about it, then?"

"Who wants to be charged as a disturber of the peace?"

Ernestine raises her hand in the air. "I've been charged for disturbing the peace ten times. It's not so bad. It's just a week of your life in a cell each time."

Brock is not impressed. "What will keep me from being charged for disturbing the peace, Father?"

Father claps Brock on the shoulder. "You can't say anything publicly until you win the senator seat."

"There is no guarantee that I will win."

"You have 50% of the popular vote, I hear."

Brock puffs out his chest with pride. "Yes, I do, supposedly. Anyway, continue explaining your plan."

Mother jumps in. "We have a mentor on the inside of the complex who has been against the system from the start. She has spent her life trying to help those inside have a better life. She helped Elira and her friends escape. Her name is Maxine."

My friends all nod at me.

"She paid us a visit the other day, and told us that since the escape, they are heavily medicating all residents 10 years of age and up to have no hormonal urges and to obey commands without question. They work with no pay until they die. Maxine says that before the resident improvements that started 30 years ago, the average life span of a complex dweller who started working at age 10 was 32 years."

Everyone leans back in shock, muttering to each other. "After the resident improvements happened residents didn't start working until age 18. Their life spans were much longer, more like 60 years."

Greggory shakes his head. "That is still disgraceful."

Father pipes in, "I have a friend on the burying committee, and he says that the people he buries are usually young children, under age five."

Brock looks down at his hands. "Why are most of them so young?"

Father squeezes Brock on the shoulder gently. "The severely disabled usually die within the first three years of complex life. My friend thinks they are poisoned because they will never be able to work, so why waste time and resources on them?"

Greggory looks like he has something bitter in his mouth. "Government sanctioned murder?"

Mother huffs, "Why not? It's government sanctioned kidnapping in the first place."

Brock rolls his eyes. "It's a law to protect the people, Mother, not kidnapping."

I can't imagine how they worded this law so people didn't know they were voting for kidnapping. "Do you have a copy of the complex law, Brock? I would like to read each word for myself."

Brock picks up his briefcase and pops it open. "Yes, actually. I have a copy of every law in here." He hands me several pieces of paper, and I immediately start reading.

Avra speaks up from the sofa. "They were going to send me to the death doctor in less than a month from our escape. I didn't seem strong enough for a job, so they were going to get rid of me. That's why Elira hurried the escape along." Scott grabs a box of tissues off the kitchen counter and joins Avra, who is getting emotional, on the couch.

I am shocked at what the ripple effect of the Complex Law is as I read it. "It says here that citizens are not able to leave the country unless they have a document signed and sealed by a mayor or higher government official."

My father nods. "Yeah. The healthy elderly and families of the deformed would flee the country otherwise."

I scratch my head trying to understand. "What keeps people from fleeing in the night?"

Father sits back in his chair. "There has been a wall and armed guards keeping us all inside the United Cities' border for 150 years."

"You've never left the country?"

"Nope."

"What about you, Brock? You are a mayor with a seal."

"I've never left the country. I've thought about it, but Chantilly likes what we have here."

"That makes one of us," I mutter as I keep reading the details of the Complex Law.

Brock holds up a cookie. "Did Complex Catering make these?"

Mother's jaw drops. "No, of course not. I have never bought a single thing from Complex Catering, or Complex Clothing Design, or Complex Cleaning Supplies. I know who makes that stuff with no choice in the matter, and no pay. I hired the best cook in the city for a reason."

My father interrupts, "Anyway, Maxine has agreed to wear a hidden camera, and take video of everything that goes on in the complex. She'll get the death doctor, the medicated food, the factory workers, the severely disabled being buried, and much more. I think the United Cities would be outraged if they knew what really goes on in there. The parents of taken children are probably already upset, and the video will bring thousands more to our cause."

Greggory shakes his head. "The general populace doesn't feel sympathy for people with health problems anymore. We're out of practice."

Mother looks at Greggory and points to Avra. "Have your feelings of sympathy come back since you've met Elira and her friends, Greggory?"

My brother looks at me, then Avra, who smiles weakly at him, and then down at his hands. "Well—yes."

Mother nods. "Good, because we need you to figure out a way to sneak the video onto the airwaves at your work once it's ready."

Greggory pushes away from the table. "What? I will get fired. This is my first job, and I like it. My boss will smear my name into the dirt. I'll never get a job again." His hand drifts to the pocket with his first paycheck in it.

Mother looks at my brother with all seriousness. "I will pay you ten years worth of wages if you do this, Greggory. I think once the complex revolution starts, you will be surprised how many people will want to hire you."

"My boss will be disgusted with me. I like him. I hate to betray his trust."

I understand where Greggory is coming from, but we need him if we are going to save Shasta and Bryon. I turn to my brother. "Could you scoot over a little bit, Greggory? My healing toes need a little bit of room to stretch."

He looks at me, and I know what he is thinking about.

I whisper so only he can hear, "Don't you want to make a difference in people's lives?"

Greggory looks at me with a straight face. "I will think about it."

My mother smiles at him, "After the world knows what is going on in the complex, we need a politician to propose disbanding the Complex Law." She looks at Brock pointedly. "That's where you come in, Brock."

"Do you know that my wife yelled at me for an hour before I left to come here? She does not want me to risk my reputation for this cause."

My father looks at Brock questioningly. "Did she read the report that came with the ult—"

"Yes Father, she did. She—still cares about the social structure that this country is built upon more than what that report says."

Mother bites her lip and shakes her head. "That is the saddest thing I've heard all day."

Father takes a deep breath. "Brock, she is in the minority. Most people don't like sending their children to the Complex of Undesirables nor their aging parents to the Complex for the Elderly. We can vote to disband the law if you write it up."

"I don't know about that. The only people who complain

to me about the Complex Law are psycho-extremists. If the complex video doesn't stir the majority of people to action, proposing a law change will be committing political suicide."

Greggory scratches his head. "Wait, did you just say that the—"

Father opens his eyes wide and shakes his head. "Not now, Greggory."

Mother takes Brock's hand. "I'm asking you to look beyond your personal aspirations and help us save lives, Brock. Can you imagine your sweet sister here dying at your age from overwork and under-stimulus?"

Brock squirms in his seat for a while. "If the video brings the revolutionary awakening you think it will, I will consider it. If no one cares, I won't do it."

My mother doesn't seem concerned at all. "Oh, the video will work. I promise you. Great, it's all settled. Maxine is meeting me here in a week. I will have a camera ready for her by then. She'll need two weeks to video everything, we'll need a week to compile the perfect mix of footage, so in one month, our revolutionary video will be on the air. Can you be ready in a month, Greggory?"

Greggory lets out a long breath. "Uh, well, yeah, if it all really comes together."

Brock looks at a calendar that he pulls from his briefcase. "But, the election is in a month. I thought I wasn't supposed to do anything until I'm elected, which still may not happen."

Mother leans sideways to look at Brock's full calendar. "You're right. We'll air it the week after you're elected, so five weeks."

Brock shakes his head. "Wow, I can't believe we're even considering this."

Mother places a hand on Brock's arm. "Imagine a better world for your children, Brock. You can make that happen."

Brock rubs his eyes. "I don't know if I really believe that this is better..."

I stand up and walk around the table to kiss Brock on the forehead. "I guarantee you, it is always better to give people more freedom."

Chapter 17

"ELIRA, CAN YOU HEAR THAT?"

My eyes are closed but I can hear a beautiful sound coming from upstairs. "Yes, that's my mother playing the piano," I say as I lift my head off Garth's shoulder.

"It's so—peaceful."

I open my eyes and look at Garth's serene face. "It is. Would you like to go upstairs to hear her play?"

Garth opens his blue eyes for just a second. "No. I can hear it just fine right here." He guides my head back to his shoulder. We both shut our eyes and enjoy the music.

I snuggle into his side. I'm feeling as cozy and peaceful as I've felt since moving out of the complex. "Garth, have you ever heard of a date?"

"It's a day on the calendar."

I laugh into his shoulder, but I don't open my eyes. "No, Maxine told me about this thing she sometimes goes on called a date."

"Yeah, what is it?"

"It's an activity a girl and a boy do to get to know each other better."

Garth speaks into my hair, "So, it's like what we're doing right now."

"No. I think the boy and girl get more privacy than this."

"Hmm."

"Hey, Garth. Want to go visit Mom and Dad today?" Jefrey asks loudly from behind us.

Yeah, I'm sure people on dates are supposed to get more privacy than this.

Garth doesn't open his eyes. "No. Not today."

"Why do you get to decide everything for both of us?"

Garth opens his eyes. "I don't."

When I open my eyes and sit up, Jefrey is sitting across from us in an armchair. "Let's count the ways, shall we? You decided we should leave the complex, you took the girl we both liked, you won't let us go to Mom and Dad's when I want to go. Remind me why I should like you again?"

Garth sits up and takes his arm back from around my shoulders. "Jefrey, I'm sorry you haven't gotten your way lately. That doesn't mean that I'm trying to ruin your life."

"Let's go to Mom and Dad's then. I think everyone in the basement could use a break from you and Elira's mushiness." I blush with embarrassment.

"Huh, let's ask. Hey, Rocky, are Elira and I bothering you?"

Rocky looks over from the computer desk. "Nope."

"Scott, Avra, are you bothered by Elira and me cuddling on the couch?"

Avra is sitting on Scott's lap at the table, feeding him truffles that she and Freda made this morning.

"Uh, no," Scott says with his mouth full.

"Nope," Avra answers cheerfully.

Garth shrugs at Jefrey. "I think you're imagining things, brother."

"I can't take this anymore." Jefrey stands up and leaves the room. We hear him slam the door to the boys' room.

"Garth, what are we going to do about him?"

"Do we have to do something?"

"He's miserable watching us be happy. We can't separate ourselves from him. It makes me feel kind of bad for him."

"He needs to get over it, but I know what you mean. I'd be mad if I were him, too."

Rocky speaks up from the computer desk, "If he had stayed

in the complex like he wanted, he would be medicated and over Elira by now."

That reminds me of a story that Rocky promised to tell us. "Hey, Rocky, how did the complex's medicine feel, by the way?"

Rocky swivels around in his desk chair and stretches his arms. "It felt... numbing."

"Avra was totally different on it than you were. Why?"

"I think it was because I knew what they were doing to me and I fought it. The other people thought the medicine was helping them and took it gladly."

Avra and Scott come over and join us on the couches. Avra pipes in, "It was definitely numbing. I didn't believe Elira knew what she was talking about until I'd had some normal food for a couple of meals."

"Where were you when they took you away for those days, Rocky?" I ask.

"On administration inspection day they put me in a tiny closet-style room with a cot and a desk. I'd been in that room a couple of times before. I used to be a troublemaker." Rocky pauses and winks at me. "This time they didn't feed me my evening—dinner. The next morning, they brought in a blueish tray and set it on the desk. I knew what was in it, so I didn't even touch it."

"I bet they loved that."

"Yeah, Mentor Briggs came in after a half an hour and pulled the top off the tray to tempt me with the smell. It didn't tempt me at all. An hour later, Mentor Briggs and Mentor Jim came in and tied me to the cot. The ties were tight. I still have rope burns." Rocky shows us red marks on his arms.

"About an hour later, Doctor James came in with a big syringe and injected me with numbing water, as I called it." Rocky mindlessly rubs a spot on his arm. "They came back in an hour and showed me four pictures. They were of beautiful women, handsome men, delicious desserts, and math problems. They asked which picture I liked the best. I knew it was some kind of test so I told them I liked the chocolate cream pie picture the best. They didn't believe me. Mentor Briggs punched me in the stomach and left."

"A few hours later Doctor James came in and injected me with numbing water again. They showed me the same pictures and asked which one I liked the best. I knew the women and the desserts were the wrong choices for their test, so I said I liked the men best. Mentor Briggs called me a liar and punched me again. I was pretty uncomfortable at this point. I had to pee, I was hungry, thirsty, my rope burns hurt, my bruised stomach hurt, and I was losing to the numbing water. It would have been so much easier to just give in to it. The third time Doctor James injected me I stopped caring. I peed myself and the answer they were looking for was obviously the math problem. So I told them it was my favorite picture. Doctor James looked at me for a minute and said to Mentor Briggs, "I can't tell if he means it, or if he said it out of process of elimination.""

Avra scrunches up her eyebrows, "I became obsessed with desserts on the pink trays. Why did they say that was the wrong answer for you?"

"I think the medicine is supposed to make girls like desserts and boys like homework."

Ernestine's voice bursts out from behind me, making me jump. "Sexist monsters."

"Anyway, the next day I was famished. I ate all three blue trays they gave me. That night they became confident that I was a zombie and started talking about secret things in front of me. Mentor Briggs and Mentor Jim said they would put us all on blue trays if they could. They said we should start working earlier too so we won't cause them as much trouble. When they let me out, Mentor Briggs punched me one last time in the gut and whispered, 'This was your last warning, dissident. One more strike and you'll be sleeping in the hill.'"

I remember what Rocky looked like when I talked to him on the phone right after this. It makes me cringe. "It makes me sick to think of everyone in the complex 10 and up on medicated trays. Poor Shasta and Tessa."

Rocky looks at his hands. "And Bryon."

Ernestine clears her throat. "That's why we had the meeting yesterday. We have to stop this unnecessary cruelty."

We all look at each other. Yes. Yes, we do.

Chapter 18

I KNOW THIS HAS TO BE A DREAM because Shasta and Tessa are here in the great room laughing and drinking fruit punch with Avra, Garth and me. I hope it's not though. "How did you guys get out?" I ask them.

"You got us out, silly."

"I did?"

"Yeah. You marched right in the glass dorm and hauled us out, knocking down mentors along the way."

"Happy Birthday, Elira!"

"Shasta, what's a birthday?"

"Honey, it's Mom. It's your birthday!"

I sit up in bed confused and disoriented. "Where did Shasta go? Why am I in bed?"

"You must have been dreaming of Shasta, darling. But now that you're awake we can celebrate your special day!"

I really don't understand what my mother is trying to say. "I thought my birthday was on December 31st like everyone else in my dorm. Today is…" I look at the calendar on my wall. "June 19th."

"I remember the day I gave birth to you very clearly, Elira. It was definitely a hot, sunny June 19th."

"So we all get pie or cookies today?"

"Um, cake actually. Is that okay?"

"Yeah. It sounds good."

"You've never had cake before?"

"Not that I can remember, but maybe I have and didn't know what it was called."

Avra rolls over and rubs her eyes. "Freda and I made you the biggest, most beautiful cake in the world yesterday."

"Avra, shhh. Don't give away all the surprises."

I am fully awake now. Apparently, this birthday thing is a big deal to my mom. I better get up and enjoy all the time and effort she has put into this—day? I slide out of bed and face my mom. She shakes her head and motions to get back in. "No, no. Get back in bed. I am going to bring you breakfast in bed.

I just came to find out what you would like the most for your birthday breakfast."

"Oh." I climb back in bed and think about what would be easiest to eat in bed without spilling on my covers. "I would like bacon, eggs, and toast."

"Okay, what do you want to drink?"

"Uh, I don't want to spill."

"Don't be silly. If you spill, I'll change your bedding."

"Okay, I want orange juice then."

"Perfect. I had a feeling you'd say bacon, so Freda is cooking that right now. Eggs and toast will be quick. I'll be back in 15 minutes. Enjoy being 17 until I get back!"

I smile at my mom as she leaves. "Avra, did she just say I'm 17?"

"Yep."

"But I didn't think I was 17 until it was time to switch dorms."

"I'm guessing we all have different birthdays, but we've always celebrated together right as we were about to switch dorms."

"So I wonder if you're older or younger than me."

"Yeah. Which makes me also wonder if you're older or younger than Garth."

Which would I prefer? I don't know. I don't think it matters. "Huh, yeah. I wonder if his mom told him what his special day of birth is."

Avra starts bouncing on the bed. "I'll ask my parents which day is my birthday when I meet with them tomorrow."

"I'm back!"

Mother comes in with a big wooden tray with little legs holding my birthday breakfast on top. It won't be as easy to spill as I thought. There is a little card on the tray addressed to me. I open it and pull two things out, a stiff card and a folded letter on lined paper.

"I'll leave you alone to enjoy your notes. Happy Birthday, Elira."

"Thank you, Mom."

I pick up the card first. It is from my mother.

Happy Birthday, Elira!

This may be the first June 19th birthday you remember celebrating, but I have celebrated on this day every year since you turned one. You've always been beautiful and sweet. I have realized since you came back that you have surpassed my expectations for inner and outer beauty. You care about people and you find joy in the simple things. It is a delight to be in your presence. I knew if I asked you what you wanted for your birthday you would say you have everything you need. I would like to give you something you want though. I asked Ernestine and your friends if they had any ideas on what you would like, and they said they've heard you talking about dates. Would you like to go on a date with Garth for your birthday? I'm guessing the answer is yes, so I've arranged a magical first date for the two of you tonight for dinner. I hope you aren't too old to enjoy cake and ice cream with your parents after lunch. We've missed celebrating with you the last 14 years. This will be a birthday for all of us to remember.

I love you,
Mom

I wipe a tear as I giggle with excitement. I'm going on a date with Garth today! My mom loves me and cares about my wants and needs. That is a precious gift that I have lived without and love so much now. I open the folded piece of paper and smile when I see that it is from Garth.

Elira,

Do you miss passing notes to each other through the grate at the complex? I realize as I write this, that I do. I still have the notes you wrote me on discarded homework paper. I know I told you we had to flush them, but I couldn't make myself do it. I shoved them down my jumpsuit the night we left. Now we can write more.

With your mother's permission, I would like to ask you on a date tonight for your birthday. I don't fully understand the significance of birthdays yet, but your mother assures me that I need to make this day special for you. I am happy to do that. I'd like to pick you up at your room at 6:00. We will be going somewhere formal which means you should wear a dress and I'll wear a suit. I'll have you back to your room by midnight. I guess this date stuff means we get to stay up late. It will be fun and full of surprises. Happy Birthday, Elira.

My life changed for the better the moment I saw you through the glass.

Thanks for choosing me,
Garth

Lifting the paper to my nose, I can smell a whiff of Garth's scent on it. I used to call that scent manliness, but I know now that it is just Garth. Jefrey, Rocky, and Scott all have their own scents and theirs don't appeal to me nearly as much as Garth's does. I wonder which came first, the affection for the boy or the enjoyment of his scent.

"So, what is making you smile so much?" Avra asks.

"I am going on a date with Garth tonight."

"Really? That's the thing you were telling me about, where a girl and a boy spend time getting to know each other, right?"

"Yep!"

"That sounds fun. Where are you going?"

"Uh, I don't know for sure, but we are going somewhere formal. Will you help me get ready?"

"Yeah. Should we do that now? When are you leaving?"

"We're leaving at 6:00 tonight. I want to at least pick out a dress and maybe a hairstyle right now though."

Avra's eyes light up. "Okay, I know just the one."

We enter our huge closet together and walk straight to the dress section. "What do you think of this one?" Avra asks as she holds up a long, silky, navy blue dress with diamond looking stones all over the front and a surprisingly open area in the back.

"It's beautiful but the back is so—open."

"It doesn't show that much skin, I tried it on the other day."

"If this is a favorite of yours, I don't want to take it."

"I'm too short for it, so don't worry. I think you should wear it with these heels." Avra holds up the most blinging pair of high heels in the closet. The shoes appear to be made of only sparkly diamonds.

Avra watches my reaction, so I smile bigger than I feel. "Wow. They are stunning. I don't think my toes can handle them, though."

"Oh, right." She frowns for a second then picks up a pair of black flats with a border of sparkly stones around the foot holes. "These will work. You should wear this necklace with it, too." The necklace she holds up has three different strands of sparkly stones. The center of the necklace has big stones and they decrease in size as they travel up the strands to the clasp.

"Do you think these are diamonds?"

"Who knows. Even if they aren't, you will be the shiniest girl on the street." Avra hands the necklace to me.

The weight of the necklace surprises me. "Do you think it's wise for me to go somewhere standing out this much?"

"I doubt you'll leave the house. I bet your date will be upstairs."

"Oh, yeah."

"HOW DO YOU LIKE the chicken salad sandwiches, Elira?"

I smile at my eager mother. "They are heavenly. The grapes add the right amount of sweet and the celery adds the right amount of crunch to the chicken."

"Do you want another croissant?"

"Uh, I've had three already."

Mother giggles. "Well, maybe you should leave room for the cake. I'll go get it."

A minute later my mom and Freda appear at the bottom of the stairs with a four-layered white and purple frosted cake. "Everybody, help me sing," my mother calls out.

"We don't know any songs," Avra says with concern.

My mother's face falls then perks back up. "I'll teach you the birthday song. It's simple."

Avra obviously wants to please my mother. "Okay, if you say so."

My friends lose their skepticism as my mom teaches them the simple words of the birthday song. "Happy birthday to you. Happy birthday to you. Happy birthday, dear Elira. Happy birthday to you!" Their song and happy faces fill me with joy. This kind of treatment sure makes a girl feel special.

My dad has his camera ready. "Make a wish, Elira, and blow out the candles."

I have so many wishes, how will I choose just one? "Do I have to say it out loud?"

"No. If you say it out loud, it won't come true," my dad assures me.

"Oh. Okay." I think my wish in my mind and blow out all 17 candles on top of the cake.

My mom claps excitedly. "You blew out every candle in one breath. That means your wish will come true."

"I hope it does."

Avra leans toward me and whispers, "What was it?"

"I'll tell you later."

Mother holds up a knife. "Who wants a piece of cake?"

Everyone wants a piece of the beautiful cake. The inside is chocolate with a red goo in between the layers of cake. I have no idea how they put the goo there. I'll have to ask Avra tonight.

"AVRA, I'M NOT SURE I should wear this. I like looking so much older but I'm afraid I'll spill my food on the silk and ruin it." I bite my lip as I look at myself in the big bathroom mirror.

"Take smaller bites and you'll be just fine."

"I really wish I knew what we are doing tonight. What if we go somewhere outside?"

Avra powders my chin one more time to cover my perspiration. "Your parents will make sure you're safe. Don't worry."

Knock, knock.

Avra almost drops the powder case she's holding. "It's six o'clock! Garth's here, Elira. Let me help you put your lipstick on." Avra slides a beautiful plum color across my lips. If my eye wasn't under a layer of makeup right now, my lips would probably match my eye.

I take a deep breath and open the door. Garth is standing there wearing a white shirt, a black suit and a black bow tie. He's wearing his fake earlobe and sideburns. Wow, his hair is gelled, and he looks amazing. I'm guessing I look okay too because he cannot take his eyes off me.

"Elira, you look fantastic."

I look into the eyes that I love, even though they're brown tonight. "Thank you, you don't look bad yourself." I tremble slightly as I take Garth's offered arm and walk with him down the hall to the great room. Everyone is looking at us and smiling, including my parents. Well, not everyone. Not Jefrey. I don't know where he is. My mom and dad are both dressed formal and fancy too.

Mother shows me the four tickets in her hand. "We are going to the opera, Elira. Do you know what that is?"

"Uh." I think of all the lessons Ernestine has given me. "It's singing, right?"

"Yes, it's singing that only a few singers in the world have a big enough range of voice to execute. If you have any of my musical genes in you, you'll like it."

I look at Garth's smiling face but then lower my gaze to his deformed hand. "Won't people notice Garth's hand?"

My dad shakes his head. "You will have a private box seat and the crowds will hide small details like a hand."

I let my eyes linger on the breathtakingly handsome man next to me. He doesn't look worried. "Okay. Here goes nothing."

ONCE WE GET TO THE GARAGE, we climb into a dark purple car with a sun roof and leather seats. I haven't noticed this car before. I wonder if it's new. The car ride to the theater is rather quiet. I wonder if everyone is as scared that someone will recognize us as I am. I decide that if I hold Garth's deformed hand in mine it will be less noticeable. When we get to the theater we get out and someone gets in the car and drives it away. "He—he's stealing your car!" I say to my dad in his ear.

He smiles at me and says, "No, he's just parking it for me. Don't worry. Smile and act like this is a normal activity for you."

Garth laughs at the look on my face which makes the corners of my mouth turn up a little too. I need to loosen up and enjoy this even though all these people make me nervous. I whisper into his ear, "Help me look natural."

He leans over and kisses my cheek. "You look like you belong with these fancy people, Elira. Just smile and everything will be fine."

A tall thin man in a tuxedo approaches us. "Doctor and Mrs. Hamble, it's nice to see you at the theater again. Who are your guests?"

"This is my niece, Edith, and her boyfriend, Garrett. They are in town for the weekend, so we thought we'd treat them to an opera. They'll take the box next to ours."

"Excellent. If you'll just follow me, I'll take you to your favorite box."

Well, that went better than I expected. The attendant looked right at my eye and didn't notice anything strange. We follow the attendant to the second story of the building. Garth and I are seated in a little room thing with soft, comfortable seats and a big open wall to see the stage down below. My parents look at me and smile as they move to the next box over. I hope they are really on the other side of this wall thing. I call around the edge, "Doctor Hamble are you there?"

"Yes, Edith, we're right on the other side of the wall," my mom's voice answers. "Sit back and enjoy the show."

I breathe a sigh of relief. Garth sits forward in his seat and looks at all the people below. "I've never seen so many people in one place before."

I sidle up next to him. "I know, and they are all so fancy."

"Eh. I have the best seat and the best-looking date in the house."

My cheeks flush. "Stop."

"I'm serious. You look great in your parents' world."

"It is..." The lights go dark in our box and the stage lights up in front of us.

I am blown away by the costumes and the voices of the performers on the stage. I don't understand what they're saying, but the music is beautiful. Garth gets a funny look on his face every time the main singer hits a high note. It makes me giggle. His hand feels so good in mine and no one out there in the dark knows that we are wanted persons. When the lights come back up we join my parents in the crowd of people going down the stairs. I wish I could talk to them but the people around us are too loud for us to hear each other.

Our car comes back! I admit, I'm glad that guy didn't steal

it. When we're safely inside my mother turns around in her seat and asks, "What did you think of the opera?"

"It was amazing. I just wish I knew what they were saying."

My mother hands me her program. "They were speaking Italian." I guess I should've looked at my own program. I hand hers back.

My dad is ready to talk of other things. "Is the birthday girl hungry?"

"Yes, I'm starving."

"I know just the place." Mother and Father grin at each other as we drive.

We pull up to a big, black, fancy looking restaurant with big windows in the front. Those windows give me some anxiety. "Mom, I don't want to be in the window where everyone can see me."

"You won't. We'll get our own rooms in the back. It will be similar to the theater."

"Okay."

Garth takes my hand as the car drives away again. My mother says this is called 'valet parking.' We hear someone playing the piano as we enter the restaurant. A man in a tuxedo is sitting at a grand piano with the top open playing a jazzy tune.

Another man in a tuxedo practically sprints to us. "Doctor and Mrs. Hamble, we are happy to see you again. Would you like your favorite table?"

"Not this time, Roman. Could we get two private rooms? Our niece and her boyfriend are in town to arrange some important financial matters with his parents. They need some privacy tonight if that's all right."

"Anything for you, Doctor Hamble. Right this way."

We are led to an elegant little room where we find a round table covered with a white tablecloth. The crystal chandelier above the table makes the fresh red rose in the center of the table glow with radiance. Garth pulls out a chair for me. The host pulls out a chair for him.

My mom looks at us like we are the cutest thing she's ever seen. "When you two are ready to go, knock on the door to your right to find us."

"Okay. Thank you, Aunt Florence." Mother flinches as she walks out with my dad.

The host places a large menu in front of me and says, "Your waiter will be with you in a moment. His name is Jeffrey."

My head jerks up from my menu. "Jefrey?"

"Is that going to be a problem, Miss?"

"Oh, no. How funny. We have a friend named Jefrey." The host smiles half-heartedly like he doesn't find that information interesting at all. He leaves with my parents and shuts the door.

Garth leans forward. "Was it just me, or did we skip the line out there?"

I look up from my menu. "Huh? Was there a line?"

"There were three other couples waiting by the skinny wooden desk when we came in."

"Oh. I hope we didn't cut in front of them."

"That Roman guy ran up to us and took us right in. I don't think he wanted us to wait in line."

"My parents must be valuable customers to him."

"Yeah, I think so."

"What are you going to have?"

Garth looks up from his menu. "I'd love to have your hand in mine."

I grin and take his normal hand in mine; he keeps the deformed one under the table. I shake my head playfully. "What are you going to order?"

"I don't know. I'm trying to decide between the prime rib and the filet mignon because they are the cheapest things on the menu."

"Oh. I think my parents would have said something if they didn't want to spend too much. I think you should get whatever you want."

Jeffrey, our waiter, enters our room with a small basket just then. "Hello, I am Jeffrey. I will be your waiter for the evening. I have been informed that the couple next door wishes to pay for your meal tonight, and you should feel free to order whatever you want. What can I get you to drink?"

My eyes flit to the list of drinks on the menu. I don't know what any of them are except one. "I'll take a lemonade, please."

"I'll have one as well." Garth says.

"I'll be back with two lemonades shortly."

"Thank you, Jeffrey." He pauses, surprised that I remembered his name.

Garth sits back and watches Jeffrey leave. "I'm still going to get the prime rib."

"That's fine. I think I'll get the salmon."

"You like fish?"

"Yeah. Especially Freda's."

"Huh. I think it's okay, but I don't love it."

"Why?"

"It's too flaky. It falls apart when I stab it with a fork. I like meat I have to sink my teeth into."

I smile and unwrap the little basket Jeffrey brought us. "I like well-seasoned flaky fish. Would you like one of these rolls?"

"Yes. Thank you." Garth looks at his white roll while he butters it then looks at me. "Elira, do you think we'll ever get to go to places like this alone?"

I sigh longingly. "Well, if we change the complex law, then yes."

"What if it doesn't change?"

I shrug. "We'll always have to live in hiding." Garth's eyes droop. Oh dang. I want to keep this conversation happy. "I think my mom wants us to experience normal life as much as possible, no matter what."

Garth lifts my hand to his lips and kisses it. "Do you think your parents will ever let me drive?"

I savor the rich buttery flavor of the roll in my mouth. "They let Ernestine drive their cars and she's a little bit scary behind the wheel, so I bet they will let you someday."

Garth flashes me one of his stunning smiles. "That would be great. That would be ultimate freedom for me. I feel like I'm always stuck in one building or another, but if I had a car and could drive, I'd never be stuck anywhere ever again."

I nod as I internalize what he said. "We did change from a life in the complex to a life in my parents' basement. But we are only stuck there because of the bounty on our heads."

Garth looks apologetic. "We do get to leave. This tonight, for example, is amazing. Don't think I'm not happy we left," he insists.

"I know. You are definitely not your brother. I just don't need a car to feel free. I like walking in the sunshine, to be honest. Ultimate freedom to me is being able to look people in the eye and not worry that they will cringe at my looks or turn me in for money. If I could do that without makeup, that would be even better." I stop talking as Jeffrey comes in with our lemonades.

"Have you decided what to order?"

Garth keeps both hands under the table as he says, "Yes. I am ready. Are you, El—Edith?"

My heart beats faster. Did Jeffery catch that? "Yes. I would like the salmon with all the trimmings."

Jeffrey doesn't bat an eye. "And you, sir?"

Garth doesn't hesitate. "I'll have the prime rib.

"Traeger style?"

"Yes, why not."

"Would you like an appetizer while you wait?"

Garth looks at me questioningly. "Sure."

"Which one would you like?"

I start scanning the menu like a mad woman for the word 'appetizers.' Garth looks at Jeffrey's notebook and asks, "What would you recommend?"

"My favorite is the blini with caviar."

Garth nods his head. "Sounds good. Is that okay with you, Edith?"

I look up from the menu gratefully. "Yes. That sounds great."

"Very good." Jeffrey takes our menus away. "I'll be back."

Garth reaches across the table and takes my hand again. "So, you're 17 today. How does it feel?"

"It feels the same as 16." I spin my fork around in a circle with my free hand then look at Garth. "Did your mother happen to tell you when your birthday is?"

He takes a long drink of his lemonade. "Yeah."

"So, when is it?"

"Why do you want to know?" Garth asks with a playful gleam in his eye.

"I want to know if I'm older or younger than you."

"What will happen if I'm younger?"

"I—I don't know. Nothing I guess."

Garth smiles as he selects another roll. "Then you really don't need to know."

That little tease. I take my napkin off my lap, wad it into a ball and throw it at his face.

Garth lets go of my hand so he can catch the napkin. "Hey, now!"

"Tell me when your birthday is!"

Garth hands back my napkin. "Okay, okay. Only because today is YOUR birthday. My birthday is May 24th."

"Oh, good."

"What do you mean, 'oh good'—you said it didn't matter."

"It doesn't."

"Here we are with some lovely blini and caviar."

"Thank you, Jeffrey," Garth says as he takes a little circle covered in orange goo balls off the tray and shoves it in his mouth. His teasing eyes never leave my face. Jeffrey leaves as quickly as he came. "Hmm. That orange goo is interesting. Try some." Garth takes a circle and puts it in my mouth.

My mouth twists around it. "It's not like anything I've ever tried before." I pick up another one and chew it slower this time. "What do you think the orange topping is?"

"I don't know. It's called caviar. It's probably a berry of some kind."

He picks up the last circle thing and takes a bite as Jeffrey returns with our entrees. My salmon looks and smells delicious. Our waiter asks, "Can I get you anything else?"

Garth swallows before asking, "My brain must be tired tonight, Jeffrey. I can't quite remember. Remind me what caviar is exactly."

"Fish eggs."

Garth's eyes bulge and he sets down the remaining half of the little circle he was about to eat. Jeffrey shuts the door and I burst out laughing. "So which do you dislike most, Garth? The fish or its eggs?"

AFTER AN EVENTFUL APPETIZER, our entrees are perfectly delicious. We talk very little because our mouths are too busy savoring each bite. "Elira, you have something on your chin, let me get it." Garth stands up so I stand up too. He leans in toward my chin and kisses me instead. Even my toenails feel the electricity between us. When we pull away I lay my head on his shoulder and smile when he wraps his arms around me.

"How do you like feeling normal, Garth?"

"Being with you is all the normal I need."

"Can you remember being separated by glass?"

He plays with my hair gently. "I could never do it again. Not now that I know what I'm missing. He guides my chin up with his finger to kiss me again. *Knock, knock.*

We startle away from each other. I find my voice somehow. "Come in." My smiling dad opens the door and enters with my equally smiley mother.

"I've already paid, so we can go if you two are ready."

I look at Garth who looks back at me like I'm the most beautiful person on earth before kissing my hand. My voice struggles to surface yet again. "We—we're ready. Thank you so much, Da—octor Hamble. It was a lovely date and birthday."

Jeffrey is waiting behind my parents and hears what I say. "Is it your birthday? I should have brought you a crème brulee on the house."

"Oh, no. I couldn't eat another bite. Thank you anyway."

Jeffrey looks at me like I'm crazy. "Not many people turn that down. Have a happy birthday anyway, Miss."

"Thank you." I should have kept my mouth shut. It's probably public record that Elira Hamble's birthday is June 19th.

My father claps Jeffrey on the shoulder as we leave. "Jeffrey, next time you're on our side of town, remember to pick up that back brace I was telling you about."

"You are too kind, Doctor Hamble. Thank you."

We follow my parents as they lead the way to the front door.

"Does Jeffrey know where we live?"

My father doesn't bat an eye. "Yes. His mother had me fit him for a back brace when he started this job 10 years ago. He says his old one is wearing out. I offered to give him a new one."

"Oh." I don't tell my father that I don't feel comfortable having him at the house, especially since Garth almost said my name and he knows today is my birthday.

Mother squeezes my arm as our car is brought back to us. "We have one stop we need to make before we head home. I hope you don't mind. Greggory needs some money to pay his rent. We're going to drop off a check to him at his work."

"Is it an hour away?"

"No, but it is a half hour away. Is that okay?"

I look into Garth's gorgeous eyes and squeeze his hand. "Sure. We're in no hurry."

I snuggle into the back seat with Garth and enjoy the sensation of his hand intertwined with mine. I'm perfectly happy in the comfortable silence of the ride until I see a gigantic building looming ahead. I sit up taller as I feel the breath leave my body and my pulse start to race. "Mother, is that—is that the complex?"

Mother turns around and reaches for my hand. "No, not quite yet. I'm sorry, I should have warned you. That first one is the Complex for the Elderly." I see a giant concrete sign that confirms my mother's story. Immediately next to the building is a large hill. I don't have to ask anything more about that hill.

I don't want to imagine how many of my friends are buried in it. Mother's eyes fill with concern as she points her head out the window and says, "Elira, that mammoth monolith up there is your complex."

I watch the building get bigger as we get closer. I can't believe how little of it I must have occupied. It is bigger than my parents' whole neighborhood. There is one light on each of the many sides of the building. My bedroom window was near one of those lights. I can even see guards dressed in white suits pacing in front of those lights. I let go of Garth's hand and start scratching my arms. Yuck. It disgusts me from the very center of my being. I feel like the aura of the complex is pulling on my soul, beckoning me to go back to where I belong. "It's not my complex," I say through gritted teeth. The matching concrete sign mocks me as we drive past; my lips barely part as I read aloud, "The Complex of Undesirables."

Garth turns my face away from my former prison. "Elira, don't dwell on it. We're out. Don't let it ruin your birthday." My body stays tense until I can't see the giant concrete work house anymore.

I let out a long breath. "Okay, I won't." Mother lets go of my hand and turns around. I take Garth's hand in mine again. "Dad, can we take a different road on the way back?"

My father's voice is accommodating and apologetic. "Yes, darling. Absolutely."

We arrive at the National News Station five minutes later.

The tension has left my body and I'm ready for the distraction my brother will bring. Greggory must have been watching for us because he runs out the door to meet us. Mother rolls the window down and hands Greggory a check.

Greggory gapes at us through the open window. "Well, well, well. Aren't we looking fancy tonight? Is this a new car?"

Father shrugs. "It's Elira's birthday, and she wanted to go on her first date."

Greggory leans in to see me better. "Very nice. Where did you go?"

My mother shows Greggory the program from the opera. "We took them to the opera and to The Ritz for dinner."

Greggory bursts out laughing. He doubles over, unable to contain himself. I don't know what's so funny but he can't get a grip on himself. He moves his hands from his knees to the roof of the car to brace himself. He finally finds words. "You took—two teenagers to the opera and The Ritz for their first date?"

Mother looks confused. "Yes..."

"You two are so—I'm not going to say it. Next time, instead of taking them to your favorite places, take them bowling or miniature golfing with pizza afterward."

I don't know what he is talking about, but it sounds fun. I think my dad is mad or embarrassed because he starts rolling up the window. "Have a good night, Greggory." Greggory is still laughing as he waves and walks back to the news building.

My parents are quiet for a few minutes as we get back on

the road. My mom eventually clears her throat. "I'm sorry if the opera was boring for you. I was hopeful that you would like it."

I reach over the seat and squeeze her shoulder. "I did! Thank you, Mom. This has been the best birthday ever."

She looks down and fumbles with her purse. "Well, it's the only birthday that you can remember celebrating, so that isn't saying much."

I can't let her feel bad about the date. "I liked getting dressed up and seeing all the people and performers tonight. Don't be sad."

Mother turns around to look at me. "You are the most easygoing daughter a mother could have. I think Greggory has a point though. The next date you have will be more age appropriate. I forget how fun it is to be young and—wild."

Dad takes Mom's hand. "They are still wanted people, honey. I think we did the best we could tonight to give them a new experience without too much risk." Mother squeezes Dad's hand appreciatively.

We pull into the garage and Dad shuts off the car. We sit in silence for a moment. "What do you think of this car, Elira?"

I look around the inside of the car. "I think it's nice."

Dad takes the key out of the ignition and hands it to me. "It's yours. Happy Birthday."

I am in complete and utter shock. I just sit there with my mouth gaping open looking at the key in my hand. Garth nudges me. "Say something."

"Thank you! I can't believe you just gave me a car. I don't even know how to drive!"

Father smiles at me. "We gave your brothers their first cars when they were 17. I'll teach you how to drive. I have a friend who owns 100 acres of land on the desert south of here. I can take you there to practice on private land. It's the best I can do."

"Thank you!" I jump out of the car and open my dad's door to give him a hug. I give Mom a hug right after that. They seem just as happy as I feel. I will never forget this night.

Garth smiles at me and looks at my key. "Will you let me drive it someday?"

"Yes!"

Garth fingers the little key with his big hand. "You need a keychain like Ernestine's so you don't lose this. I'll make you one."

"Thank you, Garth."

Everyone else is in bed when we walk in. Mom and Dad give me one last hug and whisper, "Happy Birthday," as they walk up the stairs.

Garth walks me to my bedroom door. "Can I give you a goodnight kiss?"

"Yes." The word is barely through my lips when his lips find mine.

Our foreheads stay touching for just a moment after we pull away. "Thank you for going on a date with me, Elira. Sorry if my breath is a little fishy."

We both crack up. I cover my mouth so I don't wake anyone up. "Good night, Garth."

"Good night, Elira."

I slip into my room and close the door. Avra is sound asleep but she left the lamp on the bedside table on for me. I see a folded-up piece of paper on the ground. I pick it up and unfold it. It's a letter.

Elira,

I'm sorry I didn't know it was your birthday until later. I hope it was all you wanted. I hope you're happy with him. Happy Birthday.

Don't forget me,
Jefrey

Chapter 19

THE SOAPY SUDS IN THE SINK feel rejuvenating as I wash the lunch dishes by hand. The dishwasher upstairs is broken, so I want to wash all the household dishes by hand, even Cook Freda's. She dirtied a lot of dishes on my behalf yesterday and I want to pay her back. Mother insists that if I'm going to wash that many dishes, then she's going to dry them. Freda is helping Avra make cookies to take to her parents' house tonight as we speak.

"I haven't dried dishes for years. It's kind of fun when you have a daughter to do it with." Mom smiles and bumps me with her hip. "How did you like your birthday and your date?"

I hope my face shows the happiness I felt the whole day yesterday. "I loved it, Mom. Thank you. I can't believe you gave me that beautiful car. I never in my wildest dreams thought I'd own a car. You are such a wonderful person and I'm proud that you're my mom."

Mom blushes at the praise. "You deserve the world, darling."

I carefully wash a sharp knife with a soapy dish rag. "Mom, I feel—anxious today. I'm not sure why. It might be because so much of our revolutionary plan hinges on my brothers following through. I'm not so sure they will."

"I think they will. Greggory has been inspired by you, Elira. He wants to make a difference in the world. He told me himself before he left the other day."

"I have seen a huge change in him. I'm less worried about him than Brock."

"Dad was there when Chantilly had her ultrasound. He saw something that makes him believe Brock will be anti-complex soon."

I hand the knife carefully to my mom. "Oh no. That is terrible news."

"It's sad that there is a defect, but defects can help build character, don't you think?"

I think about that for a second. "Well, mine have. I guess you're right."

"Sometimes I wonder if Chantilly or Brock had a physical flaw, if they would be more— Anyway—"

"Mom, there's another thing on my mind. Are you nervous about Avra visiting her parents tonight?"

"Yes, I am."

I wipe my hands on a dishtowel. "Do you think a parent would sell their child for $100,000?"

"I wouldn't, but I've never tasted poverty, so I don't know how tempted they will be."

"I feel terrible because I told Avra that the rest of us can't go; it's too risky. She was a little bit disappointed, but I think she understands."

"Ernestine will drop her off at six. I just hope she's there when Ernestine comes back to pick her up at nine."

I throw a wet dish rag into the sink in exasperation. "I can't believe we're questioning her parents' love. This is crazy. I'm sure she'll be fine—Right?"

"I—I'm glad you believe in them."

"I'm just trying to be optimistic."

I PLOP DOWN ON THE BED next to Avra. "Are you ready for tonight?"

She shrugs. "My cookies turned out nice. Will you braid my hair?"

"Sure." I walk over to her side of the bed and start picking through her hair. "You'll be outside at 9:00 tonight to be picked up, right? Oh, and don't let Ernestine drive home immediately if you think you're being followed. Try to lose them."

"Yes, I know. We've been over this a million times."

I feel bad that I've been hounding her so much. I just can't shake this terrible feeling. "I bet your sister, Roselle, will love you like she's never loved anyone before."

"I hope so," Avra says quietly.

"You don't seem excited."

Avra squeezes a pillow to her chest. "I am. I'm just nervous."

You and me both, my friend.

I finish her hair, then leave her to nap before the party with her parents. As I exit our room, I see Jefrey walking out the door by himself with some dollar bills in his hand.

I approach Ernestine. "Why is Jefrey leaving the house by himself?"

"He wanted to go buy a bag of potato chips at the convenience store. He said he wanted the chance to get it right."

I smack my forehead with my palm. "Since when do we allow people to leave the house alone for frivolous reasons?"

"We've been letting Scott visit his parents alone the last

week, and the convenience store is closer than that. I don't see what the big deal is."

"Is Scott at his parents' house right now?"

"Yes..."

"Did Jefrey bring up Scott when he asked permission to go?"

"Yes—Why?"

Knock, knock. I rush to the hidden door behind the bookshelf. Rocky, Garth, and Avra are right behind me. We click the door into place and press our ears to it. Garth smiles at me and puts his arm around me. "You seem tense."

"Yeah. I am." The voice we hear belongs to Rocky's dad, Frank. False alarm, I guess. Ernestine lets us out.

Frank smiles at us and admires the handiwork of the hidden door. I cringe inside. We don't know him well enough to show him our ultimate hiding place. Ernestine, what are you thinking?

Frank puts one hand on Rocky's shoulder, and the other hand on Garth's shoulder. "I need to borrow some muscle today. Are you two men up for hauling some plywood for me?"

Rocky and Garth look at each other then turn to Ernestine. She sees the pleading in Rocky's eyes and nods. Garth says, "Yeah, sure. We can do that." I let out a huff of breath. Garth looks at me curiously.

Frank nods. "Do you have time now? When we get it all done, I'll order pizza. How does that sound?" I huff again. Frank turns to me. "Do you want to come, young lady? Your girlfriend can come too."

Avra shakes her head instantly. "No, I am meeting my family on Roller Street today."

I mentally slap myself on the forehead. I don't want to go either. I just think we're getting a little bit too casual around here. "Frank—is it okay if I call you that?" He nods at me. "We have a bounty on our heads; we have to be careful."

He smiles at me. "I know, I know all about the bounty. I'll take good care of these guys. Are you going to come?"

I shake my head. "No, some other time. Thank you."

"All right, time's a wastin'. Let's go, boys."

I hug Garth a little bit longer than usual before he leaves. He still seems puzzled by my nervous reaction. I don't have time to explain. Garth signs to me as he leaves. *Don't worry about us. I love you.*

I freeze to my spot as those three little words change my whole being. Mother closes the door and looks at me curiously. "Was that sign language? What did he say?"

I giggle and head to my room. "Just—something."

When I get to my room, I don't notice that Avra has followed me. She has to say my name five times before I respond. "Elira! Will you help me get ready or not?" Oh, yeah. She's visiting her parents. I look at the clock: 5:00—time to focus. Avra needs to leave in half an hour. I help her pick out a loose pink top with some skinny fitting black pants and help her do her makeup. I start daydreaming of Garth's voice saying the words I can't stop thinking about while I'm putting powder on Avra's cheeks. "Elira! That side is done. You're going to make me look lopsided. Give me that." She takes the powder away from me and finishes her makeup herself. That was probably a good choice because she looks amazing. I grab my key and insist on going with Ernestine to drop Avra off. I don't want to sit around by myself all night.

Ernestine looks tense as we turn down Roller Street. "Avra, don't tell your parents anything that will help the authorities find us."

"I know. I won't." Her dad is watching out the window as we pull up in my purple car. Why did I insist on taking this car? He's probably writing down the license plate number as we speak. As Avra walks up to the door with the plate of cookies that she made, the door opens and her father calls out, "Where are your friends? I told you to bring them too."

I see Avra shake her head and I'm sure she's making excuses for us. Two females who look like Avra, except poorly dressed and one is older and one is younger, appear at the door and swallow her up.

"Ernestine, they love her, right?"

"Yeah—in theory." She doesn't convince me.

As Ernestine and I get home, I try not to feel bad about not going to Avra's party. I want to support her; I just can't shake the feeling that something is wrong. Ernestine opens the door for me and the first thing I see is Jefrey sitting at the table eating from a big bag of potato chips.

I explode at him. "Where have you been?"

"I bought this bag of chips at the convenience store."

My eyes glower at him. "I see that, but you should have been back before we left. What else did you do?"

"I just had a nice conversation with a guy at the store. Is that a crime?"

"That depends on what you talked about."

"Back off, Elira. Your parents may own this house, but no one owns me."

"I never said I did..."

My mother walks into the kitchen just then. "Elira, I've been meaning to take you shopping to get a few things. You have a few hours before Avra and your other friends get back; why don't we go now?"

"I-I who will stay with Jefrey?"

Ernestine looks at me curiously. "I will. Don't worry, I'll keep him out of trouble."

"Fine, just give me a minute to check my raccoon eye makeup."

Wow. I don't know what has come over me, but I have got to calm down. I can tell by the looks on everyone's faces that I am being over-the-top concerned. I go into my bathroom and take a few calming breaths as I touch up the flesh colored makeup on my long, purplish birthmark. I put some lip gloss and fake glasses on. I don't think I look like an escapee. I walk out of my room completely ignoring Jefrey, and waltz out the door with my mother. I hope I can stay calm and enjoy this outing with my mom. Wait. I feel a smile creep onto my face. Garth loves me, so of course I can.

Chapter 20

MY MOM LOOKS SIDEWAYS AT ME from the driver's seat of her white sports car. "I hope Jefrey deserves the interrogation you just put him through."

I sigh. "Probably not. I'm just on edge about Avra today. I'll try to relax and enjoy this time together. Where are we going?"

"I thought we could go to the salon and get pedicures and manicures. We didn't get very much time alone together yesterday, so this will make up for it."

"Okay, what is a pedicure again?"

"It's something moms and daughters do together. Your feet will love it!"

"Well, how can I refuse, then?" It is surprisingly relaxing and rejuvenating to have someone soak and rub expensive creams into my hands and feet. A lady with bright pink and blue hair paints my fingernails silver and my toenails purple. I feel like such a fancy, beautiful woman. I wonder if Garth will like them. The woman looks at my eye many times and doesn't notice a thing. I remember my conversation with Garth last night and sigh. I was right. This is true freedom. When we're done, I try not to gasp when I see how much my mom is paying for all of this.

We climb into the sports car and head to my mother's favorite restaurant. The outside of "The Dish You Wish" is beautiful. It looks like it is made of crystal with cozy multicolored lights inside. An impeccably dressed waiter meets us at the door. He says that the reservation list is full, but for Florence Hamble, his favorite guest, he can find something. I guess that means that my parents hold clout everywhere in this city. I try not to look nervous as the fancy people around me watch us be seated.

"Florence, I haven't seen you at our favorite haunts in months. Where have you been?" a thin, middle-aged woman with completely white, yet stunning, hair asks my mother from the table next to ours.

"Hello, Adelia. I haven't been out and about much

because I'm redecorating my basement, helping Brock with his campaign, and this weekend, hosting my sweet niece here. Edith, this is my friend, Adelia Burmingham. Adelia, this is my niece, Edith Westergard."

I smile at the stunning woman. "I'm so pleased to meet you, Mrs. Burmingham.

Adelia smiles at us both. "I can see the family resemblance. That is a lot on your plate, Florence. I'm glad it's you and not me. Good luck with everything."

"Thank you, Adelia."

I pick up the menu with shaking hands, and realize I only know what three things on it are. Mother whispers to me, "You handled that very well, my dear. You are a natural. The Veal Parmesan is to die for by the way."

"That sounds wonderful; I'll order that."

"Just so you know, Edith, I gave Maxine the camera yesterday morning before you woke up. She may have started videotaping the goings-on at the complex. Our plan is already in action."

I look around at all the people looking at us. "That's good but let's not talk about any of that stuff right now. Let's just talk about things that don't matter, like fingernail colors and cute shoes."

Mother looks at me sideways. "Ha, ha, ha. Okay, do you think the shoes I'm wearing tonight are cute?" I look at her shoes and nod.

We laugh and joke through dinner and the whole ride home. It feels so good not to worry about anyone or anything. I should give myself a break more often. Plus, Garth loves me. I look at the clock in the car: 9:45. Avra should be back!

I rush inside to see how Avra's party went. When I open the door, I have a smile on my face and my fingernails ready to show my best friend. Instead, I see Jefrey slumped in an easy chair with a hand covering his face and Ernestine pacing the great room, with tears rolling down her cheeks. They are watching the news on the television. A picture of Avra in handcuffs is showing next to a man announcing that "tonight, one of the six escapees from the Complex of Undesirables has been apprehended." I sink to the floor. "Avra Brown was taken from her former parents' house on Roller Street in Herrington today at 6:30 pm. The individual who alerted the authorities about where Brown would be tonight wishes to remain anonymous in the hope of turning more of the escapees in. The individual did receive an award of $20,000 and the authorities claim they will pay the same amount for any of the escapees still at large. Here is a picture of the five who remain at large and their names." I can't move. I am in complete shock.

My mother grabs Ernestine's arms and demands, "What did you do? What happened?"

Ernestine wipes her eyes and nose on her sleeve. "She wasn't outside at 9:00 when I went to pick her up, but there were six peace officers and their cars with the lights flashing instead. I didn't know what to do, so I just kept my eyes forward and kept driving past. I came home and fretted until the news came on. I saw that they took her almost the same time you did."

"AHH!" I sprawl on the floor bawling in earnest now. I knew something was wrong. Why did I let her go?

My mother sinks to the floor and wraps her arms around me. "It'll be okay, Elira. There was nothing that you could do." She turns to Ernestine, "Are the other boys back? Where are they?"

Ernestine covers her eyes with her hand. "Th-they're not back yet. I don't know what to do! What if they were all taken? What if the peace officers are coming here, next?"

Knock, knock. "Get in the bunker now! Even you, Ernestine," my mother whispers loudly and urgently.

Jefrey, Ernestine, and I all run to the hidden room. Ernestine collapses on one of the couches and cries into her arms. Jefrey and I listen at the door.

"What happened to you? Why are you so late?" my mother yells.

A male voice answers, "An officer came to the door, so I had to sneak out the back, and slowly sneak back here. I had to hide for almost an hour in a trash bin."

"I'm sorry that happened. Go take a shower and get some clean clothes on. We can talk more when you're done."

Jefrey seems intrigued. "I'm pretty sure that is Scott out there. It sounds like he got away from a peace officer."

I wipe the hair out of my teary eyes. "I'm so glad. I just hope Rocky and Garth are okay." A tear slides down my cheek, but I wipe it away quickly as I see Jefrey glaring at me.

"Elira, do you think she's going to let us out now?"

"No, I don't. I don't think she'll let us out until Garth and Rocky come home."

"But what if they don't come home?"

I slap Jefrey across the face. "He's your brother! Act like you have a heart, Jefrey."

He touches the red spot on his cheek in surprise. "Hey! I have a heart. He could be totally fine. I'm just wondering if we're going to have to sleep in here tonight."

"Why don't we just plan on it. Hop into a bunk and go to sleep," I say as I lay on the floor next to the door. He tries to sit next to me, but I glare at him and point at the bunks. He walks to the closest one and pulls the blanket and pillow off the top bunk. He drops them on me. I pull the blanket off my face and scowl at him. He gets the hint and tucks himself in the bottom bunk for the night.

I lay on the floor for an hour. It was actually nice of Jefrey to give me the pillow and blanket, but his insensitivity toward Garth and Rocky cancels it out, in my opinion. The floor is hard as a rock, but I don't want to miss anything, so I'm staying here. All I can hear is Ernestine's sniffling, Jefrey's loud breathing, and my mom's quiet mumbling. I think Jefrey's right, it must be Scott out there. They talk back and forth after he gets out of the shower, but they are too quiet for me to know what they are saying. I hear some sniffling out there after a while. Scott must know that Avra is gone. Those are hard words to accept. Will I be hearing the same words about Garth? Please—please no. Don't let him be gone. I can't cry anymore. I'm all cried out. My head hurts. Maybe if I just close my eyes for a little bit, I'll be able to think better.

Chapter 21

I WAKE UP TO SOMEONE SHOVING ME in the side. Ow. What gives? Oh, I fell asleep in front of the door. I need to get out of the way. My mother's head pops through the crack in the door. "Elira, wake up. Move out of the way. I have some breakfast for you."

Everything from last night comes flooding back to me. I try not to start crying as I roll out of the way. "I don't want breakfast; I want Garth."

My frowning mother and a red-eyed Scott squeeze

through the door with a tray of waffles and fruit as I try to crawl out of their way.

Mother sets the tray down on one of the beds and sighs. "What a night. You will have to stay in here from now on, everyone." Mother looks at Ernestine, who is slumped on one of the couches not looking at anyone. "Garth and Rocky are not back yet." Ernestine makes a whimpering noise. "The fact is, we should probably assume they were taken too."

I go from crawling on the floor to holding my knees in the fetal position. I scream more than cry. The last thing Garth said to me, or signed to me, was that he loved me. I didn't even get the chance to say it back. Now he will never know. The final doctor will kill him. He won't betray me, so they will kill him.

Ernestine pounds the arm of the couch like it is responsible for taking her only son away from her again. "I am going to kill Frank! How stupid was I to let him waltz back into our lives after all these years."

Mother sits next to Ernestine on the couch and pats her hand. "We don't know for sure that it was Frank. The peace officers may have shown up at the right time and taken them all."

Ernestine jumps to her feet. "Let me out of here, Florence. I am going to that house of nightmares right now. If Frank is there, I am going to kill him. We told him too much. If he's not..."

Mother stands up and grabs her friend's shoulders. "No,

you're not. The peace officers will be watching that house closer than ever. I can't lose you too."

Ernestine sits back down and bawls. "It hurts worse this time. I had him back. I know and love who he has become. I could only imagine who he was before."

I wipe my eyes and scoot across the floor to Ernestine. I lay my head on her lap and hug her legs. We bawl together for a few minutes. When I raise my head back up, I see that Scott is suffering on the other couch alone. I join him on the couch and cry with him too. "How could we have been so foolish? We've done so well for all these months and then, BAM. Three of us are gone."

Scott wipes the tears from his eyes and looks at me. "Who did this to us?" he asks.

Jefrey hands Scott and me plates of waffles and fruit. He clears his throat. "It had to be Avra or Rocky's dad. They are both poor and have nothing to lose."

Ernestine stabs a strawberry with her fork. "I bet it was Frank. Someone has to go check on that house. Florence, will you go?"

Mother looks at her friend with pity. "I don't know. I will send someone. I just don't know who yet."

We hear a gentle knocking as my father slips into the room with us. "I will go check on Frank, but not until some of the five peace officers leave our street. I am afraid they will follow me."

Mother taps her fingers on her knee. "Isn't it food basket night at the church?"

"Yes."

"Maybe you should take some food baskets around to the poor and—take one to Frank too." Mother looks at Ernestine hesitantly.

Ernestine shrugs. "That's as good a plan as any."

Mother stands up and collects our breakfast dishes. "I'm so sorry, everyone. If you can think of anything that will help you pass the time in here, just let me know."

Ernestine looks at me sadly, which makes me start crying again. "Florence, will you bring the chess board in here? I'm going to go crazy locked in here all day thinking about—Rocky."

"Yes. Absolutely. Anything for you, Elira? Scott? Jefrey?"

The boys shake their heads. I can only think of one thing. "Can I have some paper and pencils, Mom?"

Mother kisses my forehead before she leaves. "Sure thing, honey."

I KNOW IT WILL DO NO GOOD, but I want to write Garth one last letter. I want to pretend like he is going to come through that door any minute, and I won't waste a single minute letting him know that—I love him too. As I kneel next to the bottom bunk that Jefrey slept in last night, I start writing with all the feeling I possess.

> *Dear Garth,*
>
> *I can't believe you are gone. We were just learning each other's birthdays and eating caviar for the first time two days ago. I loved that time we had, just the two of us, laughing about nothing and holding each other. When the sight of the complex filled me with anxiety, you knew just what to say. You are the one who makes me feel safe and happy and loved. When you signed those three simple words to me, I felt something change in me. I felt like the world was good and right and that I would always be happy. I wish you were still here. I want to feel all of those things again, and most importantly, I want you to know that I love you too.*

"Who are you writing to?" Jefrey asks as he looks over my shoulder.

I fold the paper in half as quickly as I can before Jefrey can read it. "It's none of your business."

Jefrey sits on the bed next to me. "Did it really say 'Garth' on the top of that letter? He's gone, Elira. You need to accept that and recognize the options that you have left."

I feel the tears start streaming down my cheeks as I fold the letter to Garth as lovingly as I can. "The only option I have today is to mourn him. Leave me alone."

Jefrey's eyes fill with frustration as he watches me put the letter in my pocket. "I am his twin, Elira. You fell for us both, and I am still here."

"You are nothing like him."

My father interrupts us as he walks into the room. "I am on my way to do some charity work tonight. I will stop by Frank Moore's house to find out what I can. Florence and Freda are bringing your dinner down in just a few minutes. Would any of you like a sleeping pill for tonight? You've all been through so much in the past 24 hours, I think a solid night's rest would do you all some good.

I immediately raise my hand. "Me. Please, Dad."

My father opens a pill bottle and hands one tablet to me. He kisses my forehead and whispers, "I'm so sorry, honey. I wish I could help you more."

My eyes fill with tears again as I hug him. Ernestine and Scott take a pill as well.

"Who's ready for lasagna and breadsticks?" My mother asks in an overly-happy way as she and Freda walk in with our dinner.

I eat, but I don't taste anything. I take the pill my father gave me as soon as I'm done with my bird-sized portion. I can't take anymore today. My boyfriend and my best friend are gone.

Chapter 22

I FEEL MY WARM BLANKET leave my face. "Elira, wake up."

I pull the blanket back up angrily. "No."

"You have to wake up. I have a surprise for you," my mother says in her much-too-cheerful voice that isn't convincing me of anything.

Days of anguish erupts out of me when I yell, "I don't want a surprise! I want Garth!"

"Then today is your lucky day, because here I am," Garth says as he walks in with a tray of bacon and eggs.

"Garth!" I scream, as I jump to my feet and throw the silver tray out of the way. I wrap my arms around him as tears run down my cheeks. How can this be? I'm so glad he's here and okay. I whisper forcefully in his ear, "I thought I lost you, and I didn't get to say I love you too." When I let go of his neck, I raise up on my toes and kiss him harder than I've ever kissed him before. I realize after a while that everyone is watching us.

"Ahem." My mom clears her throat. "Could you two let Rocky and I past you, please?"

I hear Ernestine's voice ring out behind me. "Rocky!"

I take my lips back and wrap my arms around Garth one more time. Over his shoulder, I see my mom tapping her foot, so I make us hug-walk to the side to let her and Rocky through.

Ernestine jumps to her feet with tears streaming down her face and hugs her son so hard, I'm pretty sure his feet leave the ground even though he is twice as broad as she is.

"I will be back with a broom and dust pan," my mom says as she kicks some egg off her shoe.

Scott walks past us as Mom brings in the broom and dust pan. His eyes are red, and he looks like he hasn't slept a wink despite the sleeping pill. I let go of Garth long enough to give Scott a hug. Jefrey claps Rocky and his brother on the shoulder briefly. He is the only one of us keeping his emotions in check.

Garth and I clean up the breakfast tray mess as my mom clears her throat. "Frank just brought these two home. He has been under constant surveillance since the boys arrived to help move the plywood."

Ernestine looks at Rocky and then at my mother questioningly. "So, does that mean Frank isn't the traitor?"

"I think he's looking more innocent than he did yesterday. We need to come to grips with the facts. I think we all know that Avra was taken by the authorities while at her parents' house two days ago. This is horrible news for her, and for all of us. The next question I must ask the group is, why did this happen?"

"Why? Why else? Somebody wanted the money," Rocky says angrily.

"Okay, maybe it was about the money, but maybe not. Then the next question is, who?"

"It's obvious, isn't it?" Jefrey says. "Her parents were as poor as they come. They turned her in for the $20,000. In fact, Avra's dad told her to bring all of us with her. It has to be him." Most of us nod our heads as we consider that.

I interrupt the group reverie. "What happened to the rest of you guys the last two days? I thought they had taken you all."

Scott rubs his red eyes. "I think you already know, Elira, but a peace officer barged into my parents' house two nights ago. I had to sneak out the back door and make my way back here slowly and carefully. There were peace officers on the streets from there to here for hours. It was almost like they knew the path I would take to get back here. I sat in a garbage bin for an hour just to be safe."

"We know officers stop by all of our parents' houses from time to time. It was probably a coincidence that you were there that time," Jefrey proclaims.

I'm not so sure. "Maybe." I turn to the boy that I now realize I can't live without. "What happened to you, Garth?"

Garth looks at Rocky and lets out a long breath. "An officer came to Frank and Ernestine's house at about 8:00 two nights ago. We had to hide in a hidden compartment in the coat closet for three hours while the officer searched the house and interrogated Frank. There were two pizza boxes sitting on the coffee table, so the officer wasn't convinced that Frank was alone."

Rocky adds, "When Dad finally let us out, we had both passed out from locking our knees, according to Dad, and a lack of fresh air. It took him a while to get us both back to normal. He said there were two peace officers watching the house so we couldn't leave."

"We spent the night hoping we could go home in the morning, but one of the peace officers came in to check things out again after breakfast. So we hid in the closet for another three hours."

"Did you pass out again?" I ask in horror.

"Yep. Plus there was still a peace officer car outside the house, so we still couldn't leave."

Garth squeezes my hand. "Your dad showed up last night with a charity basket and told Frank that he'd take the officer out to breakfast in the morning so we could get away. It worked, and now we're back."

I hug Garth again, enjoying the warmth and strength I missed. I just want to know why this fiasco happened in the first place. "We still have a traitor."

Ernestine pipes up, "I'm not so sure it was Avra's dad."

"Really? Who do you think it was?" Mother asks.

"I don't know for sure, but I don't think he knew where Scott, Rocky, and Garth were going to be two nights ago, yet officers showed up while they were there."

"Like I said, it was probably a coincidence. My mom says officers stop by every so often," Jefrey insists.

I think Ernestine has a point, but I don't want to fight with Jefrey again right now. I look at my friends and say, "It may have been Avra's dad and two coincidences, but what if it's not?"

Chapter 23

I AM HAPPY TO HAVE PERMISSION to take a shower. Garth probably gagged when he smelled me this morning. I'm surprised how shaken I still am as I lock myself in our—my room. I see Avra's cast-off shirt on the floor. I pick it up, hold it to my face to catch her scent, and start to cry without tears. There is no moisture left in my body. I want my best friend back. She was the main reason we escaped in the first place. I can't imagine what they must be doing to her. I remember what they did to Rocky and he didn't even have information on escaped dissidents. Her heart can't take this much trauma. What if her heart just gives up? I can't believe I failed her. I should have stayed with her. I could have—taken out six officers? No, I couldn't. I hate to say it, but if I had stayed, I would be back at the complex too.

I am going to get her back. I have no reservations about the revolution plans anymore. It has to happen, and it has to happen as soon as possible. I start thinking about the phases of the plan. Maxine is doing her part right now. I can trust her; that part will work. Phase two: make the video. My mom and dad say they can do that. I believe them. Phase three: do I trust Greggory to sneakily put the video on the air? I hope so, but I don't know. Phase four: Brock proposes to change the law. I hope that about half of the population is against the complex, but is it slightly more than half or slightly less than half? We need to start creating sympathy for our cause. If it takes a year to pass the law, will Avra be okay that long? I will have to decide if we wait for the law or break my friend out first.

Come to think of it, maybe I should make a list of possible traitors. If one of my brothers is the traitor, then this plan is doomed.

Possible traitors: Avra's dad Greggory and Brock, but they didn't know she would be at her parent's house that night. Frank did though. Avra blabbed the street name and everything right before she left. He had a lot of information. Jeffrey from the restaurant. He may have figured out that Edith and Elira have the same birthday and have a history of staying with the

Hambles. I think he would have sent officers here though, which didn't happen. My parents and Ernestine. I have to put them on the list because they know everything that goes on around here, but they helped us escape the complex, so I don't think it is one of them. All of us escapees. It's obviously not me, but Garth and Rocky were gone a long time. They wouldn't turn us in for money, would they? No. They were my number one and number two supporters when I wanted to break out. I don't think it's either of them. Scott and Jefrey were alone for quite a while that night too...

I put my list to the side. I'm not sure what else I can do. I take a quick shower, thankful to send my dried-on tears and body odor down the drain. I leave my bedroom determined to find the traitor. Garth is waiting in the hallway for me. He embraces me. "Are you all right?"

A sob escapes my lips. "Not really." He gently presses my head to his shoulder and holds me for a while. "Garth, for the first time since we escaped, I feel exposed and vulnerable."

He strokes my hair. "Something is definitely not right. I can't figure it out though."

My head pops up. "I am trying to figure out who gave Avra up. Will you help me?"

"Yes. Should we get Rocky to help us?"

"No. Just you and me for now."

"Okay..."

"Let's lock ourselves in the bunker while everyone is showering so no one can hear us."

"I like that idea."

"Garth, this is serious."

"I know. Sorry."

Once we're locked in the bunker, we sit on one of the couches to talk traitors. "Were you and Rocky with Frank the whole time? Is there any chance that he is the traitor?"

"Rocky and I were with him the entire time. He even had the pizza delivered to us so he wouldn't have to leave us alone." Garth kisses my hair and then pauses. "I guess he was on the telephone in the other room when he ordered the pizza that first night. I didn't hear the conversation, but I really don't think it was him."

"What about Scott? Do you think his sadness is genuine, or do you think he is faking it to cover his tracks?"

"I'm pretty sure his sorrow real. He would never give Avra up."

I look into the clear blue eyes that I love and hate myself for asking, "You wouldn't turn her in for $20,000 would you, Garth?"

He pauses. His eyes betray the hurt he's feeling, and he lets go of me. "No way. Don't you know me? I would never do that to a friend."

"Would your brother?"

Garth pauses again. "I—I don't think so. He is a prick, and

I can hardly stand the sight of him lately, but I don't think he would do that."

"I wish I knew that."

"He seemed really worried about everything a few minutes ago. I don't think he would betray us."

"Well, that leaves Avra's dad then."

"I guess so."

I remember the shabby house and furniture that Avra's family has. Her Dad was nice but something seemed off. "Part of me thought he would do something like this when I met him, but part of me thinks that his love as a parent should stop him from doing such a selfish thing."

Garth tentatively puts his hand on mine. "It's a strange world out here, Elira. It's so hard to tell what people are going through and what they will do when they are having a weak moment."

I love the warmth of his hand. "I'm going to have Ernestine drive out there to see if there is any sudden change in circumstances at the Browns' house."

"That's a good idea."

"Would you do me a favor, and keep an eye on Scott and Jefrey?"

"Why?"

"I know they both were out alone last night before Avra left for her party."

"I will, but I don't think I'll find anything."

I glower at him. "Please, Garth. I want to feel safe here again."

"Okay, I will," he says as he guides my chin to his for a kiss.

Chapter 24

MOTHER SAYS WE CAN SPEND ONE NIGHT
in our own beds, but we have to be on high alert and expect
to spend most of our nights in the bunker until we figure out
who the traitor is. The next day Greggory stops by to see me.
He finds me writing down information I know about possible
traitors on sheets of paper at the table in the basement. "Hey,
little sister, I haven't let Mom know, but I am really having
second thoughts about this plan."

I throw my hands in the air. "No, Greggory. Not now! Not
after they have taken Avra!" I feel the tears start to form.

He looks confused. "What? They took Avra?"

"Yes, she went to meet her parents, and when we went to pick her up, the authorities were all over the house. We saw her on the news. Don't you watch the news? You work at the news station."

"Not on my days off!"

My fists automatically clench. "Yes, Greggory. My best friend is right back at the place I was trying to save her from."

He leans back in his chair at the table and looks at the sofa. "I can't believe it. We were all just here having that meeting."

My fist pounds the table. "That's how quickly life can change when you have a deformity. We may as well call it life with no rights."

He runs his hands through his messy, blonde hair. "I like Avra. What can I do to help?"

I resist the urge to roll my eyes. "Stick to the plan. We have to get her out."

He seems truly distressed by this news. I don't think he is the traitor. "I-I okay. I will do it for Avra."

"Thank you, Greggory."

He looks at my list of possible traitors. "You can just cross me off right now, young lady."

I twist my lips as I look at him. "Okay, but only because you're still helping us."

Greggory touches Brock's name on my paper. "I hope

Brock really does his part. His biggest sponsor is very pro-complex. It's going to be hard to defy him."

"What about his wife?"

"She is very pro-complex too. She's a social climber and she doesn't want to fall off the top of the ladder."

"Have they had any doctor visits lately?"

"Yes, actually. They've had quite a few lately. Why?"

"I-I just hope nothing is wrong with the baby. I wouldn't want him sent to the complex."

"Yeah."

I wish I could spend a day in Greggory's shoes. He gets to work in the news and talk to all kinds of people. He has no idea the knowledge he has at his fingertips because of his ability to wander the town as a free man.

"Greggory, from the news and the people you talk to, do you think Brock has a good chance of winning the election?"

"He has an excellent shot. He is leading in the polls by 55% right now. When I go anywhere with him, women want him to kiss their babies, and men want to shake his hand. Even when I'm not with him, almost everyone I know talks about voting for him."

I nod. "Oh good. It's hard to tell from in here, what the world thinks."

"He lacks in many areas when it comes to awesome brother-ness, but he knows how to smile and get people to trust him."

"He is cocky, but I hope he'll do the right thing."

"I hope so too. So, where are the twins at?"

"Garth is talking to Scott in their bedroom, and I'm not sure where Jefrey is."

"So tell me about you and Garth."

My cheeks heat up. "I don't think that is any of your business."

"I'm pretty sure my only sister is my business. Does he treat you right? Or does he use you for what he wants?"

I continue to blush. "He is kind, thoughtful, and treats me amazingly well. He's quiet and not pushy, which I love about him. He lets me be me and loves me for it."

"It seemed like Jefrey couldn't keep his eyes off you the other night either."

"Yeah, the choice was obvious to me."

"It's not obvious to me. Why did you choose Garth over Jefrey?"

"It wasn't a hard choice once we left the complex, and I could see and talk to them both on a daily basis. Jefrey cares about Jefrey which I find very unattractive. I want someone who can see beyond himself."

"Speaking of Jefrey, I thought I saw him walking away from the house as I pulled up. I thought that was kind of strange. You guys don't leave the house alone usually, right?"

I sit up in my seat. "Right. Especially after Avra was taken.

That idiot!" *Knock, knock.* "That's probably Jefrey coming back from the convenience store."

Greggory peeks out the blinds in the kitchen window. "No, there are three peace officers out there! Hide, Elira!"

"Garth! Scott! Rocky! Shelter, now!" I whisper and gesture loudly. I pull open the bookshelf door as the officers knock harder. My parents come rushing down the stairs with Ernestine. The boys run to the shelter with Ernestine right behind them. We shut the door firmly until it clicks. Ernestine and Scott sit on a couch while Rocky, Garth and I press our ears to the door. I hear my mom telling my dad and brother, "Take a deep breath and remember that we have done nothing wrong. So act confident."

"Excuse us, Doctor and Mrs. Hamble, we have received an eyewitness account which insists that they saw people of a wanted nature on these premises. We will have to search the property." The lead officer sends his men to search in each direction. I can hear all the cupboards and closets being opened and closed. I'm sure my parents and brother are having a hard time looking calm and collected. Please, Greggory, don't say anything stupid.

"That is ludicrous! We would like to know who says there have been wanted people on the property," my dad demands.

"The guy wishes to remain anonymous."

"I'm sure he does."

Greggory sounds upset. "Don't you have to have a warrant

to search someone's home? This is invasive, and against the law."

"No, young man. Those rights were given up when the Complex Law was revamped by President Alexander Prystine."

After searching the house for 45 minutes, the officers meet back in the basement great room. "Commander, we have found evidence of people staying in the bedrooms, but there is no one here except a cook and these three."

"Where is your hired help, Mrs. Hamble? Aren't they the ones staying in these bedrooms? It looks like they haven't done much remodeling inside here. It looks practically the same as the last time I visited."

"The yard keeps them very busy this time of year. Didn't you see them out there when you came in? They might have left for lunch."

"At 10:45 am?"

"When you start your work day at 6:30, you get hungry sooner."

I worry that he is eyeing my mother down, hoping to get her to crack. She stays strong though. "Speaking of getting hungry sooner, was cook done with the coconut clusters upstairs? We should all go up and taste test them for her."

"I remember the last confectionary wonder I tried here; it was excellent. I would be a fool to turn away such an offer, Mrs. Hamble."

"You would be a fool indeed."

I laugh silently and humorlessly. I can't believe that food is enough to distract them again, but I can hear them going up the stairs. I turn to the boys and Ernestine and whisper, "I can't believe it. Someone sent them here! There is only one person who wasn't here when the peace officers came."

"Jefrey," we all mumble together.

"I'm going to punch his lights out," Rocky says.

"Are we sure it was Jefrey? What if it was Avra's dad?" Garth asks.

"Avra's dad doesn't know we're staying here." Scott insists with a hard edge to his voice.

Garth keeps defending his brother, "But Avra does. Maybe they interrogated her until she cracked."

I bristle at his statement, yet shrug my shoulders. "I don't know, but I don't think this safe house is safe anymore."

"Where else can we go?" Scott wonders out loud.

"I don't think our house is safe." Ernestine says. Garth nods his head in agreement.

"I think we need to find a place that is not connected to any of us," Rocky adds.

I remember an offer of shelter. "We could go to Maxine's apartment. She offered it before we escaped."

Ernestine seems hesitant. "That might be a good temporary place, but once the video goes live, she will probably have to go into hiding as well."

The reality of what Ernestine says hits me square in the

face. "We are doing the right thing, aren't we? I feel terrible about what we're putting our friends through."

The door opens and my parents and brother walk in. My mother looks defeated. "I'm sorry, but I think we are going to be under constant surveillance for a while. There is a peace officer sitting in a car across the street. You will have to stay in here as much as possible. Go clean up your rooms and bring your things in here."

Greggory looks at the windowless walls and bunk beds and shakes his head. "This is crazy, I will get that video on the air as soon as possible. Good people like my parents shouldn't be ostracized like this. Especially by a government that is supposed to be for the good of the people."

I brush my hair back from my raccoon eye. "It's for the good of people with no physical flaws."

Greggory stares at my birthmark. "Yeah, why are we letting people with mental and emotional flaws dictate what happens to those with physical flaws? What a hypocritical society."

Mother wraps her arm around Greggory. "We are about to fix that. We are more determined than ever, right?"

"Right," Greggory agrees.

Chapter 25

I FEEL LIKE I AM GOING TO GO CRAZY looking at the same blank walls all day. Will Maxine's apartment be any better? Where is Jefrey? Not here. Scott says that a bunch of clothes and bags are missing from their room. I think Jefrey knows that if he tries to come back here, we'll destroy him. The note he wrote me on my birthday suddenly comes to mind. *Don't forget me.* How did I not see that it was a goodbye note?

Good news comes in the form of my mother at dinner time. "Maxine dropped off video footage today."

Yay! I ask her excitedly, "Can we watch it now?"

"No, Brock is on his way. When he gets here, we'll all watch it together and decide what needs to be on the final video."

I look at Garth's feet dangling from the bunk above me. "Okay, I can wait that long." I tickle Garth's foot just for something to do.

"Ah! You asked for it, Elira Hamble," Garth says as he jumps off the top bunk and attacks my armpits.

"Ah! No! Ha, ha! I was just teasing you."

Mother clears her throat. "I wish you two didn't have to share a—room. But since you do, I insist that you stay away from each other's beds."

Garth stops tickling me and stands up straight. "I'm sorry, Mrs. Hamble. We're just running out of things to do in here. Ernestine is a good chaperone. It won't happen again."

"Even so, Garth, I'd like you to move to the bunk above Scott instead."

Garth's eyes droop. "Yes, Mrs. Hamble."

When Brock arrives, we are thankful for the chance to leave the bunker to watch the video footage. Brock seems angry and stressed when he arrives. Great, his wife probably yelled at him for helping us again. His bad mood won't help us get him on our side. This video probably won't improve his sour mood either.

I am right. Brock seems to get more and more angry as we watch cooks mixing medicine into the food at the complex and severely disabled children being hauled out and buried. I am extremely shocked to see the 16 girls in our old school room not giving the boys on the other side of the glass any attention at all. Wow. Things have changed.

I stand up when I see a tall blonde. "Wait! Go back. I think I saw Shasta." Mother backs up the tape and plays it again. "Right there, in the corner. Look at Shasta, Garth. Look at her face, and her hands." Shasta's eyes are glazed over and her long, thin hands are red and blistered.

My father speaks up. "My friends tell me that they're so heavily medicated that they don't complain when they get cuts and scrapes on the job, so no one treats their wounds."

I feel a lump form in my throat. Shasta's dead-looking eyes are permanently plastered in my memory. My poor friend. The video shows me places in the complex that I was never able to visit. I see ten and twelve-year-olds sitting at rows and rows of sewing machines making fashionable clothes that they will never get to wear. Their jumpsuits are as white, gray, and black as ever.

I see teenagers mixing chemicals and filling cleaner bottles. When one spills a harsh chemical on her leg, the leg of her jumpsuit is immediately burned through and her skin disintegrates before our eyes, red and blistered. She is given a wet rag that she holds to the wound as she cries without tears. It's strange to watch people with no emotions.

The kitchen scene shocks me. The food we were fed

was always very simple. The catering food that they make looks fancy and delicious. Those poor kids, spending their days making decadent food that they will never get to taste. They don't know that of course. They probably think that the next dorm up gets to eat what they are making. Each dorm you move up, the food does get better, after all. It keeps residents from asking why the things they make aren't used by themselves. The complex management is horrible, but they are smart. When we see a close up of a ten-year-old boy pouring hot, liquid plastic into a mold with blistered fingers, Brock absolutely loses it. He stands up and screams and pulls his hair.

My parents and friends look at my brother in shock. I'm pretty sure I know who that ten-year-old boy reminds him of. I jump up and hug Brock. He hesitantly puts his arms around me at first, then hugs me back, tightly. "Are you okay, Brock?"

"The complex is worse than I thought. I can't believe you lived like that for 14 years, Elira."

I pat his arm. "It has gotten worse since I left. Those poor people."

"I-I've been in and out of doctors offices all week. They have all confirmed that our baby has a serious defect. I can't send my baby boy to the complex. He has a heart condition. It doesn't matter if I become a senator. By law, my son will be sent to the complex when he is two. I hate it. I want to watch my boy grow up in our home. It's so wrong."

I look into his eyes. "That's why you must help us. Change

the law, Brock. Change it for Shasta, Avra, and your innocent baby boy."

"Chantilly doesn't want me to. She says that our baby shouldn't live with us if he can't keep up with us. I never realized that she cares more about how people view her than about her own family's well-being."

Mother shakes her head. "She's wrong, Brock. She'll realize it when she sees your son's sweet face."

He rubs his hair in frustration. "I hope so. I was still unsure of what to do as I drove here today, but now that I've watched this video, I am convinced you're right, Mom. The complex law has to go."

My mother jumps off the couch and hugs him. "I know what you're feeling and I'm so proud of you for doing something about it."

He looks sad and defeated. "I—I have to."

My dad is shutting down the television when my mom stops him. "Wait, Ross. Greggory told me that the advertisement that he has been working on for Geronimo's Germ Away is supposed to air on the news tonight, lets watch it."

"Okay. Let's see what our boy has done." My dad finds the national news channel and we all sit back and watch who was robbed by whom and what the government's take on the upcoming holiday is, when breaking news hits.

"This just in, a second escapee from the complex of

deformities has been apprehended tonight." We all gasp and look at each other.

"Jefrey Yesterly was the person responsible for the capture of his fellow escapee Avra Brown last week. He gave additional information last week insisting that it was accurate information that would lead to the capture of two or three others. That information proved to be unreliable. Tonight, Yesterly gave the authorities the address of where he claimed the escapees' safe house was located. That information proved to be inaccurate as well. The head officer on this case began to be suspicious of Jefrey after he was sent on a second day of false errands, so he took Yesterly in for questioning. It was revealed that Yesterly, also known as Jack Dodge, had large purple blotches all over his body, and that he was in fact one of the six original escapees."

A scream erupts out of me, "That traitor!"

"You know, John, this story seems bizarre to me. I would think that the escapees would stick together, not turn each other in."

"That's what I would think too, Sally. It just goes to show that money can turn even friends into traitors."

Garth gets up and starts pacing the room. Scott walks to the television that still has a picture of Jefrey on it and hits Jefrey's digital face. "I can't believe he did that to her. And me! I hid in a garbage bin for an hour! He sold us all out. So Garth, are you with him, or with us?"

I can tell Garth is insulted. "I'm not with him. Don't you

guys know me at all? I am fuming mad. The idiot! How can he love money that much?"

Ernestine clears her throat. "I think that when Elira chose you over him, he took that pretty hard. He has been different for weeks."

Garth pounds the wall in frustration. "This is ridiculous, my own brother tried to turn me in."

I wrap my arms around him. "It's not your fault, Garth."

He looks down at his shoes. "At least his brainless plan didn't pay off. The people that gave Jefrey money to stab us in the back stabbed him in the back too."

We all fall silent. The only sound in the room is Greggory's advertisement for Geronimo's Germ Away cleaners. When it's over my mom stands up and turns off the television.

She sighs. "I know you're all upset at Jefrey. I am too, but it's done. There's nothing we can do about it. At least we know that Avra's dad didn't turn her in. We have to get Avra out before they torture or work her to death, and we have to get the law changed before they take Brock's baby boy. There's no way around it; our complex revolution begins now." All of the heads in the room nod in agreement. I am thrilled that my brothers are finally on board. Mother has one last question for us. "Who is ready to stand toe-to-toe with The Complex Chief and Alexander Prystine?

About the Author

Heather Hayes loves a good story. She believes a good story will entertain you and leave you feeling like a better person for having read it. She loves living in Idaho with her husband and five daughters. If she isn't writing, she is probably watching a volleyball game, cooking, skiing, reading, or planning a trip to somewhere new.

A Message from Heather Hayes

If you liked uncovering the complexities of the United Cities with Elira, please tell your friends about it and leave a review on Amazon; it helps me out more than you know. The last book of THE COMPLEX TRILOGY is coming soon to Amazon and HeatherHayesAuthor.com.

The Complex Life

The Complex Law

The Complex Leader (December 2018)

If you like a good story for younger readers, check out my other books:

Unexpected Magic

A Tale of Regrets

Rissy's Summer Son

The Fantastic Backyard of Imagination